# THE ELNORA MONET

ELNORA ISLAND BOOK ~~THREE~~ 4

RACHEL SKATVOLD

Copyright © 2021 by Rachel Skatvold

All rights reserved.

No part of this book may be reproduced in any form or by any electronic or mechanical means, including information storage and retrieval systems, without written permission from the author, except for the use of brief quotations in a book review.

ISBN: 978-1-951839-22-2

Celebrate Lit Publishing

304 S. Jones Blvd #754

Las Vegas, NV, 89107

http://www.celebratelitpublishing.com/

*~To my mom, Joy Davidson~*

*When I first started brainstorming for this series, I knew I wanted my first two main characters to be New Englanders like you. I love your stories of going to Nantasket Beach as a kid—drinking orange pop and putting chips inside your sandwich so they wouldn't blow away. Just like Luc's mother in this story, I'm thankful I can always count on you to give helpful advice, even though I'm grown up now with a family of my own. It is a wonderful gift to have a mother who's also a best friend and Godly role model. I hope you enjoy the little bits of New England and other special memories from growing up weaved into this book that remind me of you. Olive Juice!*

"The heavens proclaim the glory of God.
The skies display his craftsmanship."
Psalm 19:1

# 1

The cell phone alarm grated like sandpaper through Carly's blissful unconsciousness. She groaned and peeked through one blurry eye. Why would her alarm be going off at six-thirty in the morning on a Saturday? Carly slid the icon to off and harrumphed before tossing the phone on her nightstand. She grumbled to herself while flopping back onto the bed and snuggling with her body pillow. Maybe her phone was on the fritz. She attempted to think of the nearest cellphone shop on the mainland, before drifting off again.

"Carly," a voice called through her lethargic fog. "Carly…are you still asleep?" When she didn't answer, the annoying pest calling her name pulled the covers down and whacked her in the head with a pillow. "Wake up!"

"Saturday…" she mumbled through her pillow. "My sleep-in day. Buzz off."

"No, not today. I have a veterinary seminar on the mainland, and you agreed to take my house call this morning. Does Mr. Belshaw ring a bell? Big mansion…temperamental Angora cat?"

Carly's eyes flew open. The first thing she noticed was daylight streaming through the window. "What time is it?"

"Seven-fifteen. You're supposed to be there at eight o'clock sharp. He's paying us extra for the early hour."

She launched herself from the bed and dashed to the bathroom. Within five minutes she'd raked a toothbrush over her pearly whites, thrown her hair up into a bun, and made a haphazard attempt to put on some makeup. Then she rushed back into her room and changed into her veterinary uniform.

When she made it down the stairs, Kendall stood by the front door, holding Carly's favorite tumbler filled with a breakfast shake. "Here you go, sis. You know what happens when you forget to eat breakfast. I'll see you this afternoon."

Carly grabbed the shake with a quick thanks before heading out the door to the RV. With thirty minutes to drive to Elnora, she'd really have to pray to make it on time. Once on the road, she cranked up the radio and opened the windows of the RV, allowing the cooler January air to flow through her hair. It was in the fifties that morning—a nice change from the below zeros they'd be experiencing in Boston. While her older sister missed snow, she didn't mourn the lack of it at all. Living on an island with warmer weather suited Carly fine.

After passing through Hooper, she crossed the bridge to reach Elnora. The landscape became flatter and she saw a few vineyards along the way. Maybe sometime soon, she'd find a free moment to visit them, although she had been trying to refrain from drinking after her mishap on Mimosa last fall. Just visiting them didn't mean she had to try any of the wine. The whole process of making and storing the wine fascinated her. The thought of walking down the long rows of grapevines seemed romantic in a way too, even if she didn't have a man to share it with. Carly was determined to stay single for a while anyway. She needed time to think and get her life in order.

Carly obeyed her GPS when it instructed her to take a right onto Belshaw Drive. The guy had a street named after him, too?

She shook her head in amazement. Driving alongside the coast for several minutes, a large gated estate came into view.

She stopped at the front gate where a guard studied her with his dark eyebrows furrowed. When he spoke, his French accent was so thick, she struggled to understand him. "Bonjour, mademoiselle. Please state your business here. I'll need to see an ID as well."

Carly fumbled over her words as she rummaged through her bag for her driver's license and handed it to him. "Um...I'm Carly Mulligan...the veterinarian. Mr. Belshaw is expecting me for an eight o'clock appointment."

He held her ID with the tips of his fingers as if it had been contaminated before handing it back to her. "Ah, yes. Ms. Mulligan. Monsieur Belshaw has been waiting for you."

Carly struggled to hold her tongue from spouting off a sarcastic remark. "Yes, could you please let me in so I'm not any later?"

"Very well, Ms. Mulligan." The guard nodded and mashed the button to open the gate.

Carly drove through, her eyes wide while taking in the Belshaw Estate at the end of a long drive with an ocean view. The middle part of the mansion was several stories high with a gabled roof. Shorter wings were attached with gables too, she guessed about two stories high, and stretched out in a large u-shape. There was one flat part on the top of the west wing she recognized as a helipad. Carly drove closer, observing grand gardens, fountains, sculptures, and a pasture in the distance with horses grazing. She pulled into a cobblestone circular drive with a fountain in the center, and continued to gawk with an open mouth while parking the RV.

An elderly butler wearing a black suit with tails came out the front entrance and approached. "Good day, mademoiselle." He pulled out a watch on a long chain from his vest pocket, clicking his tongue. "Three and a half minutes late. We'll see if Mr.

Belshaw can still fit you in. May I call a valet to park your... um...vehicle?" he asked in a thick French accent like the guard.

Carly shook her head, peeved by his comment. "Thank you, but no. This is my mobile clinic. I might need the exam room and supplies once I speak with Mr. Belshaw."

The butler eyed the RV with a raised brow, as if the vehicle tainted the elegant aesthetics of the estate before motioning for Carly to pass. "Right this way to the parlor then. Mr. Belshaw will send for you when he has a free moment."

After the butler escorted Carly to the parlor, she attempted to calm her temper after talking with the rude butler. Her eyes drifted upward to the paintings on the walls. She walked closer, recognizing pieces by famous artists on the wall, particularly 19$^{th}$-century impressionists. Most were landscape paintings by Monet, Renoir, and others she'd studied in college.

Carly stopped by a reproduction of a water lily painting by Monet to study the variation of colors when a woman's voice interrupted. "Ms. Mulligan, I'm Mr. Belshaw's secretary, Mrs. Potter."

She turned and smiled at the middle-aged brunette woman in business attire, relieved she had an American accent she could understand more easily. "It's nice to meet you."

She offered a smile. "Likewise. Mr. Belshaw had an unexpected conference call. He asked me to take you to Descartes' wing and will talk to you afterward."

"Descartes' wing?"

Mrs. Potter nodded. "Yes, Mr. Belshaw's cat has his own rooms. Please follow me." Carly did as she asked, gazing at the elegant features of the mansion along the way. She had never dreamed of setting foot in such a grand place. Mrs. Potter led her into the east wing of the mansion and opened the last door on the left. Walking in, she saw a large room with a large cat condo, scratching posts, and walkways along the walls. Carly had trouble not rolling her eyes after taking in the cat paradise.

The room was so big it nearly took up the entire lower level of the east wing.

She found Descartes in the center of the room, on an elevated, oval cat bed with dark blue tulle surrounding it. He was a pure white Turkish Angora with one sky-blue eye and the other amber. When the cat saw her, he crouched on the bed, hissing and growling at her. She recoiled, not expecting such hostility. "Is he usually so standoffish?"

Mrs. Potter nodded with a nervous giggle. "With strangers, yes. I've only worked at the Belshaw Estate for about two years and he warmed up to me eventually. Mr. Belshaw pays me extra to care for Descartes, and I don't mind, being a cat person. All the others he's tried to hire to care for the cat have resigned… due to his spirited nature."

Carly nodded. "I would believe you on that. Does he have any favorite toys or treats I could bribe him with?"

Mrs. Potter's perfectly waxed eyebrows knitted together. "He…doesn't really play…however, I could offer him some food."

"That could work." Carly watched the secretary as she crossed the room to a compact refrigerator on top of a large marble counter. She took out a pouch of fancy organic cat food she'd seen in a commercial once. It had no preservatives and had to be kept cool to prevent it from spoiling. The moment Mrs. Potter tore the pouch open and poured it in a fancy glass food dish, the cat ran right past Carly and leapt onto the counter. "Well, at least I know he's nimble and eats well."

"That isn't exactly so," the secretary said while gently petting the cat as he licked at the food. "He'll sniff and lick it, but he doesn't eat much. That is one of the reasons Mr. Belshaw sought out your veterinary services."

"I see." Carly approached slowly, noticing the cat taking a bite, but only chewing on his right side. "Maybe he has a bad tooth." While the cat swallowed and then sniffed at the food, she saw her chance. Carly put on her gloves and caught the cat with a firm but gentle grasp on the scruff of his neck. Descartes squirmed, growled, and hissed, but she didn't give in to his display of aggression. "I'm just trying to help you," she said in a soothing voice while keeping the cat in a firm hold and opening his mouth. Sure enough, she noticed an abscessed tooth on the left side of the cat's mouth. She checked the other teeth and then looked the cat over while she had the opportunity. Overall, he seemed healthy other than the bad tooth and Carly let him go.

Mrs. Potter chuckled to herself as the temperamental feline zoomed off the counter and hid in the kitty condo, still snarling and growling. "You're good. I've never seen anyone get the better of Descartes."

Carly shrugged while removing her gloves. "I'm used to holding and examining difficult animals. It's a little easier in a clinic setting where they have fewer places to run, but I thought it best to catch him while he was distracted." Her attention was drawn away momentarily, hearing a whirring sound from the corner of the ceiling. She noticed a small security camera rotating toward her. Carly turned back to Mrs. Potter, fighting the urge to roll her eyes at the realization she was being spied on. "That tooth will need to come out, and I heard he needs annual vaccinations, but I'd like to discuss it with Mr. Belshaw first to make sure of what he wants me to do." She looked up at the security camera and pursed her lips as if talking directly to an elusive, snobbish white-haired man behind the camera. The old billionaire probably had nothing better to do than count his riches and spy on unsuspecting people. "It would be easier to do the vaccinations while Descartes is sedated for the tooth extraction."

"I'll let him know when he's finished with his conference call."

"Mrs. Potter," a deep voice called through an intercom on the wall. The man had a hint of a French accent, but much easier to understand than the security guard and butler. "Please send Ms. Mulligan in now."

"Yes, right away, Mr. Belshaw." The secretary motioned for Carly to follow her into the hallway again. They walked down the long east wing and back to the main part of the mansion. She marveled at an enormous chandelier in the middle of the double arched stairway leading to the second and third floors. When they reached the second floor, they took a right and Mrs. Potter motioned toward the first door on the left. "He'll meet with you in his office in a few moments." Carly thanked Mrs. Potter and walked inside. Right off the bat she noticed another painting by Monet. This one featured two women and children walking through a field of poppy flowers.

A door opened from the other end of the room. "Are you intrigued by the arts, Ms. Mulligan?"

She turned to face Mr. Belshaw and studied him for a moment, not expecting to see a man in his mid-thirties with dark hair and striking blue eyes behind his rectangular-framed glasses. After gathering her thoughts, she nodded with a forced smile. "Yes, I minored in art while in college. 'Red Poppies at Argenteuil' is one of my favorites by Monet. I heard his wife and son were the models for the painting."

He lifted an eyebrow. "Yes, I've heard that as well. Impressive insight. Did you recognize some of the pieces downstairs in the parlor as well? I saw you studying them."

Carly's smile faded. "So, you were watching me."

He gave her a guilty grin while sitting behind his grand oak desk. "I apologize. It is a habit of mine to study who is coming into the mansion. You see, I have a split screen computer that allows me to have video conferences, work, and view the surveillance cameras simultaneously."

Her eyes narrowed. "I see. You are the type of person who likes to control everything?"

"In a way. Yes." He motioned toward the chair in front of his desk. "You can have a seat if you wish, Ms. Mulligan."

She crossed her arms in defiance. "No, I'd rather stand, thank you. And please, call me Carly."

His cobalt eyes twinkled and his upper lip quirked in amusement. "Very well. Your choice, *Carly*. And if we're going to go by first names, my name is Jean-Luc, after my father, but most people call me Luc for short." He paused to take off his glasses and lay them on the desk, bringing out the color of his eyes even more. "I'm sorry we got off on the wrong foot. Please, would you mind telling me the diagnosis for Descartes?"

"You weren't listening in before?" He studied her for a moment, but didn't take the bait, so she cut him some slack and relaxed into the chair he'd offered earlier, feeling an obligation to make up for her unprofessional behavior. "Descartes seems to be in good health, upon my brief exam, but needs an abscessed tooth removed and his annual vaccinations. We'll need to make another appointment and Dr. Kendall Mulligan will do the procedure in our clinic."

He nodded. "I will have my scheduler call this afternoon. Is there anything else?"

Carly started to shake her head, but she couldn't hold her opinion inside any longer. "I'm sorry if I'm overstepping, but your cat seems in need of some socialization. Do you ever spend time with Descartes?"

Luc released a hearty laugh, making the corners of his eyes crinkle. She would have enjoyed the sound if not for the questions racing through her mind. "I know you've seen how temperamental Descartes is. Last time I tried to pet him, he nearly scratched my eyes out."

"Don't you spend any time with your cat?"

He nodded. "From a distance. I think Descartes prefers it that way."

Carly shook her head in astonishment. "Your cat wants for

nothing, material wise. He even has his own wing of the mansion, but I don't understand something. Why do you have a cat, when it seems like you don't even like him?"

Luc's smile faded and his eyes drifted to the clock on the wall, shoulders becoming rigid. "I believe this is a subject that would best be discussed at a later date. If you'll excuse me, Ms. Mulligan, my helicopter is arriving in a few minutes."

She nodded, the fact he'd used her last name again not escaping her notice. "Of course, Mr. Belshaw. We wouldn't want to keep your pilot waiting."

"Thank you for coming. For the record, I've never seen anyone get the better of Descartes like that. You were good with him, although I'm sure his pride is hurt."

Carly chuckled softly. "He'll get over it soon, I'm sure. Have a good day, Mr. Belshaw."

"You too."

He showed her to the door, shutting it behind her, then she followed the waiting secretary back down the hallway to the stairs, and out the front entrance. While Carly got back into the RV, she heard a helicopter whirring overhead. As it landed on the helipad on the roof of the west wing of the mansion, she caught sight of Luc running out to meet it with some attendants close behind. Right before reaching it, he turned with his blazer whipping in the wind from the propellers and gave her a little wave. Carly waved back, shaking her head. The man had managed to annoy, bewilder, and charm her in the short five minutes they'd spoken. He'd also avoided her questions in such a polite, yet infuriating way. With her outgoing personality and thirst for adventure, she'd met a lot of interesting people, but none puzzled her as much as Jean-Luc Belshaw.

## 2

By the time Kendall returned home from her seminar, Carly had just finished preparing a simple meal of spaghetti and meatballs. She set the table and smiled as her sister came into the kitchen. "How did everything go?"

Kendall sighed and relaxed into a chair, pausing to sweep a few auburn curls from her face. "It was good, but long. That spaghetti smells delicious. I'm starving."

"Well, good. I slaved over a hot stove for hours and hours to heat up these frozen meatballs."

Her sister chuckled at the sarcastic remark. "What I'm trying to say is, simple meal or not, I really appreciate you making dinner tonight. I'm so exhausted, I'll probably head off to bed right after dinner." She yawned before putting some spaghetti on her plate. "So, how was the house call today? I hope you didn't end up getting there too late."

Carly shrugged. "Three and a half minutes late, according to Mr. Belshaw's snobby butler."

"Was Mr. Belshaw upset about it?"

"No, he didn't seem to be." She chuckled softly and shook her head. "Did you know he was in his thirties?"

Kendall shook her head with wide eyes. "No, the Jean-Luc Belshaw I looked up online was in his seventies."

"Apparently, I met with his son, Jean-Luc Jr. He told me he prefers to go by Luc though."

Her sister aimed an ornery grin in Carly's direction. "So, did you find this *Luc* attractive?"

She felt heat rushing to her cheeks, but quickly composed herself. "He is easy to look at. I'll give him that, but his arrogance makes that fact irrelevant. I may have made things worse by lecturing him about not spending enough time with his cat."

Kendall gasped. "You didn't. Carly, we needed to make a good impression. He's one of our first customers on Elnora, not to mention one of the wealthiest. If he's not pleased with our vet services, I'm sure word will spread around the Islands quickly."

Carly rolled her eyes. "Oh, relax. For the most part, he seemed unfazed…even amused by me."

"Amused?"

"Yes, it was infuriating." Kendall started to chuckle until Carly punched her shoulder. "Stop! It's not funny."

"Ouch!" Her sister rubbed the sore spot on her arm, her mouth still twitching into a smile. "All right…all right. Calm down. It's just unusual for me to see you so flustered over someone."

Carly's blood started to boil. "I'm not flustered…I'm just… I'm just…oh, never mind!" She scoffed and began piling spaghetti onto her plate. "Let's pray before this food gets cold."

After his business meeting in Savannah, Luc asked his pilot to swing by his mother's beach front house on Hilton Head before returning home. As the helicopter tilted to make a turn, the mainland disappeared and the island took shape, and his thoughts drifted to the morning's events. People seldom surprised him, but the witty veterinary assistant had caught him off guard. While most people glazed over the truth to prevent hurt feelings, she had gone straight for the heart of the issue. Even the fact he came from a wealthy, high profile family hadn't seemed to faze her.

He'd grown used to women recognizing him, especially when he spent time in Paris with his father. They would hang all over him like barnacles, drinking in his words and pretending to be interested because of his name and wealth. It was why he preferred a simple life on Elnora. The gated estate allowed him to work in peace and most of the locals paid little mind to him, aside from the occasional art events he hosted. Now, those were but a distant memory. These days he preferred seclusion.

When Carly walked in with her messy blonde bun, curious blue eyes, and unique New England accent, he'd anticipated some fangirl behavior once she realized who he was. However, she had seemed annoyed by him and unimpressed with his lavish estate—besides the artwork on display. Her knowledge about Monet impressed him more than he wished to admit. Learning she'd studied art in college, but ultimately chose a career as a vet's assistant fascinated him. What caused her to have such diverse passions?

Drawing close to his mother's property, Luc shook his daydreams of Carly away. His mother would notice his absent-mindedness and start asking questions. To clear his head, he watched the coastline drift by, until her house came into view. The average person would have never guessed his mother's true wealth if the property didn't include a privacy gate and helipad. Her modest, six-bedroom cobalt house was two stories tall with a large wraparound porch and held a treasure trove of memories from his teenage years. After the divorce, she'd insisted on moving back to Hilton Head to raise him and his younger brother away from prying eyes. It wasn't until his eighteenth birthday that she gave him the keys to the summer estate on Elnora—one of the properties she'd received during the settlement. She said the memories were too painful for her to live there, but that didn't mean he couldn't enjoy it.

When he came up the steps, he was greeted by his mother's white Pomeranian named Socrates first. After patting him on the head, he found his mother in the sunroom watering some of her houseplants. Her smile lit up the room when she saw him. "Luc, I wasn't expecting you today. I thought you were busy."

He shrugged before she pulled him into a tight embrace, her head only coming to the middle of his chest. "You know I'm never too busy to come see you at least once a week, Mother."

"What did I do to deserve a son like you?"

"Are you saying I'm a punishment or a blessing?"

She chuckled and slapped his shoulder. "A blessing, of course! I'm glad at least one of my children decided to stay close, at least for the time being."

He released her, his smile fading. "Have you heard from Pierre?"

She nodded and stepped back to retrieve her watering pitcher again. "Briefly. He's been in Marseille taking the lead on that new venture for your father. I guess he met someone there…a model for one of the campaign shoots. I hope this one's nicer than the one he brought here for Thanksgiving last fall." She sighed while watering a potted hosta. "I'm guessing you've probably heard more than I have?"

He admired the vibrant fuchsia petals of his mother's amaryllis plant. "Her name is Celine. He seems happy and has been spending a lot of time with her. That's about all I know."

"That's good. I hope it works out. It's only natural as a mother to wish for my children to find happiness. Both of you." She looked up and studied his face, her eyes asking the question he didn't want to answer, but it was too late. His mother could read him better than anyone. Luc stayed silent, waiting for her to say it out loud, but she just gave him a knowing smile and turned back to her flowers. "I'll be finished in a second. Will you stay for lunch? I have leftover finger sandwiches and salad from a luncheon I had yesterday."

He agreed and a few minutes later they walked through the living room on the way to the kitchen with Socrates yipping and wagging his tail behind them. Luc paused, observing a familiar painting of the sea at sunset. In his mind, he listed off all the colors, imagining an array of paint shades on a palette.

"I hope you don't mind," Mother said, coming up beside him. "I found this in the closet in your old room. It was a piece from your senior year of high school."

He smiled and rubbed his chin, deep in thought. "I'm glad you found it. Looking at it reminds me of simpler times. Painting came so naturally."

"It's part of who you are, Luc. You have such talent."

He studied the short brush strokes he used to create the sea in the piece and shook his head. "I'm afraid my muse is elusive these days." Luc's eyes drifted to the vibrant orange, violet, and magenta in the sunset, silently criticizing his rudimentary technique from his younger years. The colors were too bright, without the drama and shadow he'd learned to add in his later pieces. Or, perhaps, it was just his current mood making the piece seem too bright and cheery? Luc couldn't be sure what disturbed him so much about the simple painting.

His mother reached to touch his cheek and tilted his face toward her. "You'll find it again. I'm certain of that. Just be patient."

Luc nodded and then broke his mother's gaze before wandering into the kitchen. They worked together setting out the large platter of sandwiches and salad covered with plastic wrap before sitting on tall stools at the counter. His mother prayed over the meal before they started eating.

He ate several of the tiny sandwiches and reached for one

more, causing his mother to chuckle. "I'm glad I had so many leftovers to feed you today. I think you would have cleaned out the fridge with your appetite. Did you eat breakfast this morning?"

He thought for a moment before shaking his head. "No, now that I think about it, I don't believe I did."

She scoffed and reached up to swipe a few stands of hair from his forehead, like she did when he was a child. "I should have guessed as much. No wonder you've been looking thinner to me. I'll have to call Mrs. Potter and make sure the cook is making you enough food."

He rolled his eyes playfully. "Mother, you don't have to nag my secretary. It's not her job to make me eat. Besides, the cook makes delicious meals for me every day. I just neglected to eat it this morning."

She nodded, her knitted eyebrows starting to unravel. "All right. It's just hard not to worry. I am your mother after all…but I'll try."

"Thank you. I know that's your job. You don't have to worry though. I forgot because I was so busy this morning. I had a few video conferences, that business meeting, and someone from the new mobile vet clinic on Elnora came to give Descartes a checkup."

His mother's eyebrow shot up. "There's a new veterinarian? What's his name?"

He wiped his mouth with a napkin, stalling. "Oh, it's run by Dr. Kendall Mulligan, but her assistant, Carly Mulligan, came out."

"Same last name? They must be sisters. It's nice to have a family owned business around. How old are they?"

His stomach tensed, but couldn't avoid her question. "The vet assistant seems mid-twenties, and I'm guessing the veterinarian is in her thirties, judging from the photo on their business card. I enjoy supporting local businesses, so I thought I'd give their clinic a try."

She nodded while straightening her placemat. "That's good. Do you have one of their business cards? I might have to check them out myself."

Luc shook his head a little too quickly, drawing a curious smile from his mother. "I believe they only offer services on the Independence Islands."

"Well, that's a pity. I'd like to find a mobile vet to give Socrates his yearly checkups, too. Maybe you could give me their card anyway and they could recommend someone here on the mainland."

Luc chuckled. "Mother, I know what you're up to. Remember that attractive blonde caterer a year ago...the one you saw me talking to at the charity benefit in Savannah? You meddled, got her number, and set us up on that blind date. It was disastrous."

She sighed while stepping down from the stool to put her plate in the sink. "I'm sorry. I have to admit, that was poor judgement on my part. She was a little loony." She rinsed off the plate and turned to face him again, leaning against the counter. "But can you blame me for trying? I hate seeing you so lonely."

He forced a smile. "I am alone, Mother, but I don't think of myself as lonely. This is good for me. I'm figuring things out... deciding what I want my future to look like."

"You mean whether or not to move to Paris?"

"Yes, there is that to consider. Father has been pressuring me to come learn the business again. Part of me wonders if a change of scenery would be good for me. I do love Paris, but do I want to live there permanently? Plus, if I go, I'll be leaving you here all alone."

She approached and touched his cheek. "This isn't about me...or your father. It's about your future. I'll support you no matter what you decide."

He smiled, feeling some of the weight lift from his shoulders. "I knew I could count on you for words of wisdom."

"And I'm glad you still seek my advice. Makes me feel useful."

He stood and hugged his mother. "Of course. I always will."

After a few moments, she stepped back, wiping tears. "Well, that's enough serious talk for now. How about some dessert? I have cherry cheese pie, your favorite."

"Sounds perfect."

# 3

Monday came all too quickly for Carly. Mr. Belshaw's secretary arrived mid-morning with Descartes. They had to sedate him before extracting the bad tooth. After that, he spent the remainder of the day recovering in one of their boarding cages. As a torrent of walk-in customers came in after that, he spent most of his time hissing and growling at them.

Carly scrambled to help Kendall with their customers. By the time three o'clock came along, business had slowed down. Carly slumped onto the bench seat in the small waiting area of the mobile clinic with her hair hanging off the side and one leg over the top cushion. Zoe, her sister's Australian Shepherd, rushed into the room and proceeded to lick her face. "Ew!" she complained and sat up sputtering. "Dog slobber."

Zoe panted happily and wagged her tail, giving her irresistible puppy dog eyes.

She wiped her face on her sleeve and ruffled the fur on Zoe's head. "Sorry, girl. It's not you I'm flustered with. I just have a love hate relationship with that slobbery tongue of yours."

Kendall chuckled as she walked into the room, observing her

rare interaction with Zoe. "Doing all right? Your head's been up in the clouds since Saturday."

Carly nodded as she continued petting the dog. "Of course. I've just been busy and have a lot on my mind." Kendall studied her for a long moment and started to open her mouth to say something else when a faint knock sounded at the door. Carly jumped up to open it, welcoming the distraction. "Annie! It's so good to see you," she said, seeing Kendall's friend from camp. She'd recently helped start a new business on the Islands, too. "Please, come inside."

Annie thanked them and climbed the stairs toting a cat carrier. "Sorry, I know you're about to close up shop for the day. I was hoping you'd have time to see one last patient."

Kendall grinned. "Of course, we have time. I didn't know you owned a cat."

Annie shook her head. "Oh, I didn't...until this afternoon. I found this sweet little one by the ferry slip. She was shivering and limping on one leg. I can't keep her, but I was hoping you could look at her leg and help find her a home on the island or recommend a nice shelter."

Her older sister nodded. "Sure, we'd be happy to help. Here, follow me into the exam room and we'll take a look."

Along the way, they passed Descartes who proceeded to even hiss and yowl at sweet Annie. She recoiled with wide brown eyes. "Wow, he's fierce!" She studied the name on his collar. "At least...I'm assuming Descartes is a boy's name?"

Carly chuckled "Yeah, he's something else. He's the most spoiled and rich cat on Elnora."

Annie chuckled nervously. "You know, I think I've seen portraits of this cat at city hall."

"You've seen portraits of this cat...like drawings?"

Annie shook her head. "No, I mean big canvas paintings. I forget the artist's real name now. He hasn't painted in a while... but they call him The Elnora Monet here on the Islands."

Carly stared at her in surprise as some of the pieces started to fall into place. "The cat's owner is Mr. Belshaw. Does that ring a bell?"

Annie grinned with recognition. "Yes, that's right! Jean-Luc Belshaw Jr. His family has owned the estate on Elnora for years."

She stood shellshocked for a moment, hearing Kendall's friend talk of Mr. Belshaw and his talent for art as if it were as common as the gulls hanging around Pirate's Cove. How hadn't she heard of him yet?

"Carly," her sister's voice called through the haze. "Are you going to come assist me?"

She blinked hard to clear her head. "Of course. Sorry." Carly held the stray cat still while Kendall examined her. She had cerulean eyes and her gray and white fur was matted with mud from being outside. She guessed, under the cat's rugged appearance, she was a senior seal point Himalayan. The cat was affectionate and purred almost the whole time, telling her she'd probably had an owner at one time or another. She only flinched and let out a low growl when Kendall examined her back right leg.

Carly held the cat a little tighter and stroked the top of her head. "It's all right. We're going to take care of you."

After Kendall finished her examination, she turned to Annie. "I think she may have a break in that leg. I'll do an x-ray to be sure. Thanks for bringing her in. I'll make sure she finds a good home and we'll foster her until then."

Annie gave her a sweet smile and tucked a loose strand of brown hair behind her ear. "Thank you. She's such a sweet girl. I wish I had room for her in my little beach house. Will you give me an update on her?"

"Sure will."

After Annie left, they got to work taking an x-ray of the cat's back leg revealing there was a break in the tibia. They gave the cat anesthesia, washed her fur the best they could, and Kendall set the break. After the cast was made, they put the Himalayan into the boarding cage next to Descartes.

Kendall washed and dried her hands before turning back to Carly. "So, since we worked later than usual, would you mind dropping me off at the house? I'll cook dinner while you return Descartes to the Belshaw Estate."

Carly groaned to herself. "Yeah, I can do that, I guess."

"Thanks for the enthusiasm, sis."

She sighed. "Sorry, it's just after lecturing one of the local celebrities of Elnora about his cat, I'm in no hurry to make a return visit. Actually, I'd rather give myself a distemper shot in the eye."

Kendall chuckled. "Just act professional. I'm sure he didn't pay as much notice as you thought. He ended up scheduling the appointment, right?"

"All right." Carly bit her lip and finished putting away a few supplies. "I'll do it, but you owe me."

Entering the Belshaw Estate the second time ended up being easier than the first. The security guard recognized Carly and her RV. He mashed the button and waved for her to go through. When she arrived inside the mansion with Descartes growling in the cat carrier, the butler led her straight to the parlor where Mrs. Potter waited. "Thank you for bringing him back. I was swamped with office work today."

Carly smiled. "You're welcome. It was no problem at all."

"Even with Descartes' foul attitude?"

They shared a laugh and she shook her head. "I'm starting to learn how to handle him and his temper tantrums."

"Nicely said." Mrs. Potter motioned for her to follow. "Mr. Belshaw is running late from his business meeting this evening, but he asked me to take care of everything. Let's talk more in Descartes' room. I'm sure you have care instructions for him?"

She nodded, relieved to not have to face Luc again. When they reached the room, she opened the carrier. The cat looked around for a few moments, sniffing the air cautiously before scampering off to a secluded hole in his kitty condo. "Well, I'm glad to see he's happy to be home." After Mrs. Potter chuckled out an agreement, Carly took out a stapled packet of instructions and handed them to her. "The tooth extraction went well, but there was some swelling around the gums. We gave him one dose of antibiotics, but he'll have to continue taking them for a week. Just mix the pre-measured packets into his food. He might not start eating better at first because his mouth will be sore, but in about a week, he should start improving. If he doesn't, or starts becoming lethargic or not drinking water, call the clinic right away."

"I will. Thank you, Ms. Mulligan. Now, would you like me to write a check for your services?"

"You can, but we find it easier to do things electronically. We would just send an invoice."

Mrs. Potter nodded. "That sounds fine. Mr. Belshaw prefers it that way actually. So, can I see you out then?"

Carly nodded, starting to fidget in discomfort. "Yes, but is there a restroom I could use first?"

"Yes, of course. The one down here needs maintenance, but you can use the one by my office upstairs. Take the stairs outside this room. It's the seventh room around the corner to the right."

"Seventh…" she said with a chuckle. "Sounds simple enough. Thank you."

"Sure thing. I'll make sure Descartes is settled in while you're gone and we can meet back here."

Carly journeyed up a flight of stairs and down the hallway, counting the doorways as she went. However, seeing the elegant statues and artwork along the way distracted her. Soon she realized she'd gone too far and had to retrace her steps. While pausing to count the doors she'd already passed, she saw a maid coming out of a room to the right. Through the open door, Carly caught sight of artwork covered in sheets, more sculptures, and a large easel. She tried not to be nosey, but the room intrigued her. Did Luc keep rare pieces in there he didn't share with guests in the house? Her mind traveled back to her conversation with Annie earlier that day. She mentioned the residents on the Islands called him The Elnora Monet. Did he keep his own artwork in there?

The middle-aged blonde woman in uniform smiled at her before closing the room behind her, concealing the objects that had piqued her curiosity. "Can I help you find something?"

Carly released a nervous chuckle and nodded. "Yes, the bathroom, please. I'm afraid I got a little turned around."

"Oh, that's not hard to do around here. When I first started working here, I got lost all the time. The bathroom is just two doors down on the left."

Carly thanked the woman and found the bathroom. A few minutes later, washing her hands turned into an interesting task. Everything was automated. She put her hand under what she thought was the water, which squirted lotion instead. With a little difficulty she found the soap. Then she put her hand under another opening which blew air at her instead of water, sending the soap flying into her face. "Well, you wicked high-tech thing!" Carly grumbled, observing bubbles and wet spots all over her clean scrubs.

After a few more mishaps, she finally had her hands washed and dried. She wiped a few rogue bubbles off her scrubs and then came back into the hallway. Carly started to head back in the direction of Descartes' room when curiosity drew her attention to the mysterious door again. She looked both ways, making sure no one was around, and then tiptoed to the door, cracking it open a few inches to peer inside. It was too dark, so Carly opened it further, flipping on a light switch. The room was much larger than she thought, with a large bay window, but she couldn't see what it overlooked because of the heavy sun blocking drapes. She glanced up and down the hallway one last time before entering the room completely. Carly inspected the ceiling, remembering the security cameras in Descartes' room; however, there weren't any in this room.

Taking in the features of the space, she saw the easel she'd caught a glimpse of earlier. Beside it there was a table with a palette, various paints, and brushes. The wall behind it was also filled with shelves of art supplies. It was a paradise, but she could tell by the stale air in the room and a few specks of dust on a few of the sheets, it hadn't been used in a long time. Carly walked to the window, pulling back one drape a few inches to peer out. Before her was a stunning view of the gardens. Why would Luc keep such a room hidden and unused? Carly started to head back toward the door, remembering Mrs. Potter waited for her, but she had to look at one last thing.

She approached the largest painting on the wall and lifted the sheet. A woman's beautiful hazel eyes stared back at her. She was surrounded by garden flowers and wore a pale-yellow sundress paired with a lace shawl and wide-brimmed hat. Everything about her radiated with elegance and grace. Yet, what drew Carly's attention the most was a pet, looking content as could be on her lap. A snow white, fluffy Angora cat. In an instant, she knew it had to be Descartes.

The creak of the door opening startled Carly. She dropped the sheet, making it slip completely off the painting before whipping around with wide eyes. To her dismay, she was standing face to face with Jean-Luc Belshaw Jr.

# 4

Luc stared into the shocked eyes of the beautiful vet assistant for a moment, speechless at first. He'd returned from his business meeting, hoping to catch Mrs. Potter in her office before she left for the day. Luc never expected to find the door to his old art studio cracked open and even more stricken with surprise, to see someone inside it. In truth, he'd thought a lot about the next time he would see Carly since Saturday, but he never imagined it would be here. Why here? Why in this place that caused him so much anguish already? The wound in his heart twisted like a knife and his first reaction was to lash out in anger, but he did everything in his power not to. He never lost his composure in front of anyone—it wasn't professional—and he wasn't about to start now. "What are you doing in here?" he asked, voice low and ragged.

"I'm…I'm so sorry. I noticed the artwork and…"

"Ms. Mulligan," he interrupted. "The rooms in this hallway are closed for a reason. I will have to talk with my maid later about why it was not locked; however, it is not polite to snoop around other people's homes."

Carly shook her head, blue eyes sparking at him. "I apologize. I wasn't trying to snoop. I was just...curious."

He calmed his temper and motioned toward the door. "Please, let's step out into the hallway." She did as he asked, her cheeks fiery red, before he followed and closed it behind them. He imagined all the pain being concealed in the room as he shut it, but that wasn't so. It was still there permeating the air like a thick cloud of smoke—suffocating him. He paused for a moment and closed his eyes before turning back to the sullen young woman in the hallway, but he couldn't make any more words come.

She peeked up at him with guilty eyes. "I'm sorry again, Luc. That was very unprofessional of me, but why would you keep a wonderful room like that hidden away? I'd give anything to have a room like that to create in."

He raised his hand to stop her, temper flaring again. "Ms. Mulligan, it is my own business why I keep the room closed. I would advise you to leave the matter alone." He pursed his lips while turning to walk away, struggling to maintain his strong front. "Now, let's discuss Descartes. That is why you stayed after dropping him off. Am I correct?"

"Um, yes," she said from behind, struggling to catch up. "I had a few care instructions I was about to go over with Mrs. Potter."

He stopped and turned toward her with a raised brow. "After you were finished exploring the mansion at your leisure, you mean?"

Carly's eyes shot fire in his direction and she opened her mouth like she wanted to aim a witty remark right back at him, but to his surprise, she held her tongue. After releasing a deep sigh, she rolled back her shoulders and stood up straight like a professional. "Mr. Belshaw, I suppose I can just tell you the instructions here and then be on my way. I wouldn't want to disturb you anymore this evening. Descartes did perfectly during the tooth extraction. He should be acting himself again in a few days, but his appetite may not return right away. I would expect him to eat slightly larger portions gradually over the next few months. I've given Mrs. Potter some antibiotics for him to take with food. If he starts acting lethargic, listless, or loses any weight, please give our clinic a call. Do you have any questions for me?"

Luc shook his head. "No, I believe you've explained everything thoroughly."

"Well, if there's nothing else, I'll be on my way. Have a good night, Mr. Belshaw."

Before he had a chance to respond, Carly had spun on her heels and hurried off in the opposite direction toward the exit. He watched her turn the corner and disappear from his sight, but he stayed rooted to the ground for several moments, as if stuck in some kind of trance. He'd been cruel and now he guessed she thought he was a jerk. Luc knew that, but she had overstepped a boundary—one that couldn't easily be redrawn.

He turned slowly, forcing his feet to retrace the hasty steps he'd taken a minute ago. Before Luc knew what was happening, his hand had turned the handle to the door—the one he hadn't stepped foot in for over two years until today. He didn't want to enter. Every fiber of his wounded heart screamed for him not to, but he had to make sure Carly hadn't disrupted anything. The maids cleaned the room once a week, to keep it free of the majority of cobwebs and dust, but they knew not to move a single thing out of place. Besides weekly maintenance, it was like a tomb—sealed, sacred, and preserved, along with the memories.

Stepping inside, he noticed the painting straight ahead of him first, with those familiar hazel eyes gazing back at him, just like the day she'd posed for the painting in the gardens. Luc could never fully capture every unique feature of his beautiful Angeline, but he'd done his best. Now, seeing her likeness on the canvas again caused a lump to rise in his throat. Even his clumsy attempts at recreating her beauty made him desperate to hold her in his arms. The smell of her citrus perfume wafted through the room, surrounding him in a brief moment of pure bliss. But a moment later, the heavenly scent left and he knew it had only been his mind playing a cruel joke on him. She was gone.

He knelt down and retrieved the sheet, before standing to drape it over the painting again. However, as his eyes met Angeline's, something made him stop. His memory took him back to that day in the garden. She stayed in the same position on the bench for about two hours. The cat had only lasted for about twenty minutes before hopping down to explore the flowerbeds. Angeline's eyes twinkled at him and her mouth twitched.

"What's so amusing?" he asked, putting the brush down to take a short break.

"You and your serious faces." She crinkled her brow and her lips pursed, playfully mocking him before giggles bubbled out of her mouth.

He grinned and shook his head. "I was trying to concentrate, and you're not helping matters with all your fidgeting."

She laughed again. "All right, I'll try to sit still for a little while longer, but you owe me."

"Will a kiss settle the debt?"

Angeline's grin grew even bigger. "Only if you pay it in full right this second."

He got up from his easel and took a seat beside her on the bench, pulling her into his embrace. They shared a tender kiss before he leaned back to gaze into her eyes. "How am I ever supposed to finish this painting now?"

She ran her fingers over his cheek with a guilty expression. "I'm sorry, did I ruin your muse?"

Luc shook his head before kissing her again. "No, *mon amour*. When are you going to realize, you *are* my muse?"

He came out of his daydream and placed the sheet off to the side. He couldn't cover up her picture again and leave her in darkness—not after remembering how beautiful she looked in the sunlight.

Carly made it all the way out to the RV before bursting into tears. It wasn't like her to cry and she scolded herself all the way back to Merriweather about it. She couldn't believe how foolish she'd been, snooping around another person's home, as Luc had put it. So much for being professional. Carly feared they would lose a customer and their good reputation once people heard. To add insult to injury, her sister would never trust her to make house calls again.

When Carly made it home, she went straight to bed, saying she didn't feel well. It was completely true. She felt sick to her stomach after her stupid mistake. She flopped down on her bed and wiped her tears, hoping sleep would take her, but it was no use. Even though her body was exhausted from the long day at work and her ragged emotions, she couldn't fall asleep.

After several minutes of staring at the ceiling, she sat up and reached for her laptop. Her fingers flew over the keyboard, doing a search online. Before long, she found what she was looking for. Pictures of Jean-Luc appeared on the screen. In one, he was standing next to his father. It was amazing how much they looked alike. She scrolled down further, discovering his father, Jean-Luc Senior, owned Belshaw Suites in Paris. The hotel franchise was one of the largest in Europe. She gasped, realizing how rich his family was. Looking at pictures of his father's estate in Paris, Luc lived a modest life in his smaller mansion.

After the initial shock, Carly spent time reading about Luc. He had an American mother, which explained why his French accent was subtle. It made her wonder how long he'd lived in the US. He was also involved in several organizations around the area. One supported budding artists and offered fine arts scholarships to college students. One organization in particular called Angeline's Wings stood out to her and she clicked on the charity website. After perusing the menu, Carly discovered the charity raised money to help animal shelters with expenses. After reading the main page she clicked on the tab marked "Dedication" and gasped at what she saw. The woman she saw in the painting at the mansion was staring back at her from the screen with Descartes in her lap. Her name was Angeline Belshaw and she'd passed away a little over two years ago.

Carly's heart sank as all the pieces came together. Descartes had to be Angeline's cat. That explained why Luc kept him even though the cat despised him. He took care of him out of honor for his deceased wife and had even started a charity in her honor. Tears pricked Carly's eyes as she continued reading about the late Mrs. Belshaw. Had everything she thought she knew about Luc been completely wrong? Perhaps he wasn't an arrogant, cold blooded, rich jerk as she had previously labeled him. Maybe it was only a mask to hide he was still grieving.

# 5

Two weeks passed by as Carly stayed busy in the vet clinic. Taking on new clients on Elnora meant they were even busier than the previous year. She welcomed the extra business though, because it kept her mind off Luc and her embarrassing behavior. That Saturday, Kendall offered to do house calls, so Carly had the morning to herself. She ate her cereal while watching the stray Himalayan cat they were fostering. They'd called her Athena temporarily and she wasted no time taking complete control over the house. Carly chuckled as she limped over in her cast to Zoe's bowl and started trying to wolf it down. The dog just watched helplessly and whined.

She walked over and scooped the cat into her arms, chuckling. "That's not yours, silly girl. You already ate all your food." The cat purred and rubbed her head against Carly's shirt. She sat in the chair again, struggling to finish her breakfast, while balancing the overly affectionate cat on her lap. She looked a lot better than when she'd come to them two weeks ago. After bathing her, the beautiful seal pattern of her fur had a chance to shine through. She was also incredibly soft. The only issue was the matted fur on her back. Next week, Carly planned on consulting with Melody Carmichael who ran a mobile grooming service on the Islands. If it came down to it, they could give her a lion cut to be rid of the mats, but then it would be a while before her beautiful fur grew out again. It might deter someone who wanted to adopt her. She hoped maybe Melody would have some tips for what to do for a longhaired cat.

Carly finished breakfast and placed her bowl in the sink when her phone started ringing. She saw her sister's face on the screen and answered. "Hey, sis. What do you need?"

"I just got a call from Mr. Belshaw. Descartes is lethargic and no longer eating or drinking. I'm in the middle of my house calls. Can you go pick him up and meet me back at the house in an hour?"

She gulped down her apprehension. Every meeting with Luc so far had been disastrous. She'd already accused him of not spending enough time with his cat, and then he caught her snooping around his private studio, opening old wounds. What would happen next? She dreaded imagining it.

"Carly, are you there?"

She shook the cobwebs from her brain. "Yeah, sorry. I can do that. See you in a little while."

Carly paced the parlor in the Belshaw Estate. She never thought Luc would ask for their veterinary services again after their last meeting, but here she was. Maybe he would be out for a business meeting this time. She could only hope.

"Thank you for coming on such short notice, Ms. Mulligan."

Carly turned around, feeling heat radiating through her cheeks. Luc was standing in the doorway, his dark hair ruffled, the top two buttons of his shirt undone, and she noticed dark circles under his eyes. It was the first time she hadn't seen him wearing a suit. "You're welcome. Is Descartes still in his room?"

He rubbed his chin and nodded. "Yes, I was afraid to move him. It's Mrs. Potter's day off and I panicked when I saw him so ill." He motioned for her to follow him.

Carly set all her previous apprehension aside and journeyed down the hallway with him. When they entered Descartes' room, the cat was on his elevated cat bed and barely lifted his head, a huge contrast from the hissing, growling animal who'd greeted her the last time. She approached and gently stroked the cat's head. He only responded with a deep sigh and started panting. "How long has he been like this?"

"I've been away on business, but Mrs. Potter said he didn't eat his food last night. Other than that, he seemed fine, but this morning I found him in this state."

Carly opened the cat's mouth, inspecting the tooth. It looked fine, but she noticed the cat's mouth looked dry. When she lifted the skin on his back and let it go it didn't have elasticity to bounce back like usual and his eyes seemed sunken a little. "I believe he's severely dehydrated."

"What can be done for that? I can't force him to drink water."

Carly nodded, pursing her lips as she took a moment to think. "Intravenous fluids would be the best way to help him."

Luc's brows knit together. "How bad is his condition? Please, be honest with me."

She sighed. "It's serious, but if we get him treated right away, he should be fine. My sister is going to meet me with the mobile clinic back at our house. Can you help me move him to the cat carrier?"

Luc nodded and gently stroked the cat's snow-white fur before looking up at her, tears welling up in his blue eyes. "Will you promise to do everything in your power to save him? He... he belonged to..." He paused and his jaw quivered. "Never mind...just please help him."

Carly nodded. "We will. Kendall is more skilled than I am in this area and she'll know what to do."

Luc nodded. "I trust you, but can I come along?"

She studied him for a few seconds, caught off guard. The desperation in his voice and eyes showed how concerned he was. Had her previous assumption he didn't care about the cat been wrong? "Of course, you can," she responded. "Would you like to follow me?"

He shook his head. "No, I'll have one of my drivers prepare the limo for us."

She nodded slowly, the thought of riding in a limo with a famous person boggling her mind. "All right, but how will I get my car? I have to work in the morning."

"Leave your keys here. One of my valets will drop it off."

She agreed reluctantly and before too long they were on their way to her house. It was supposed to be her day off. How had she ended up riding in a fancy limo across from a French billionaire and his spoiled Turkish Angora cat? It was like a scene from one of those cheesy made-for-TV movies her sister loved to watch.

Carly attempted to relax, but it proved difficult with Luc close by. The concern remained in his eyes, but his shoulders relaxed a little once they were inside the limo. "I wanted to apologize for my behavior a couple weeks ago. I'm not usually quick-tempered."

She avoided his eyes, checking on the cat in the carrier instead. "You don't need to apologize. It's me who should be doing that. I was the one who was snooping where I didn't belong. I hope I didn't disturb anything."

Luc sighed and looked out the window as they crossed the bridge to Hopper Island. "You didn't. Honestly, it was well past due for someone to let some fresh air into my old studio."

"If you don't mind me asking, why don't you use it anymore?"

He turned and gave her a sad smile. "I'm sure you may have guessed already, but the woman in my painting was my wife. Descartes was her pet before we were married." Luc let out a brief chuckle. "The cat has always disliked me. He tolerated my presence while Angeline was alive, but his hostility toward me has grown as the years have passed."

"That explains a lot. Some cats do tend to pick favorites. Since Descartes was so close to your wife, he must have grieved her loss as much as you."

Luc rubbed his chin, studying Descartes as he rested in the carrier. "I didn't think of that before."

"Animals can feel sadness and loss like people do." She paused, fiddling with her necklace before peering over at him again. "By the way, I'm sorry to hear about your wife."

"Thank you. She passed away from a brain aneurysm two years ago. It was very sudden. One day she was happy and full of life...and the next..."

She felt a lump rising in her throat. "That's awful. I can't imagine losing someone like that."

"I miss her every day, but I'm thankful she didn't suffer. She passed in her sleep."

Carly wiped a stray tear off her cheek, hearing the raw edge to his voice, even as he tried to hide behind a stoic expression. "It doesn't make it any easier though, does it? I lost my brother a couple of years back and it's still painful to talk about. We did have a chance to say goodbye, but I still wasn't prepared."

He ran his fingers through his hair and turned toward the window again. "You're never prepared to lose someone you love. I suppose in a way, keeping Descartes makes it seem like I still have a small piece of Angeline with me."

The rest of the way to Merriweather, neither of them spoke. To fill up the silence, Carly texted back and forth with Kendall about Descartes' condition. When they reached the beach house, her sister was already there waiting for them in front of the mobile clinic.

Kendall eyed the limo, but didn't say a word about it. Instead, she motioned for them to follow her inside the RV. "I've got everything set up," she explained. "Let's see what the problem is." After everyone was situated inside the examination room and Kendall looked the cat over, she shared a glance with Carly. "I believe your diagnosis is correct. I'll start IV fluids right away."

Luc stayed by Descartes, stroking the fur on his head while Kendall sedated him and started the IV. Any other time, the cat would have rejected such affection from his owner, but he was too sick to care at the moment. It was endearing to see, yet sad at the same time. It was obvious now he really did care for his pet, just from a distance usually because of Descartes' hostility. Luc looked up, while continuing to try and soothe the cat. "Will he be all right? I'll cancel my business trip to New York tomorrow if this is a serious condition."

Kendall shook her head. "I don't think there's a reason to worry. We'll start him on some fluids and that should help. I want to do some blood tests, too. We need to get down to the bottom of why he's not eating or drinking well. Otherwise this is going to happen again. How long will you be on your business trip?"

"About three days. I'll return on Tuesday afternoon."

Kendall wrote down a few notes on a notepad. "That sounds fine. I could board him until then. That will give me some additional time to observe his behaviors and get the blood test results back."

He nodded. "Thank you. Do whatever you need to. Spare no expense."

"Descartes will receive the best care, Mr. Belshaw. You don't need to worry. If we lack the resources here at the clinic, there are clinics on the mainland I know of that can help."

Luc managed a relieved smile. "Thank you, Dr. Mulligan. If it's all right with you, I would like to stay here with him for a few hours, just until he's out of the woods."

"Of course, Mr. Belshaw. That's fine with me. I'll be at the little desk in the waiting room on my laptop if you need me."

Carly stood in the corner of the room, watching Luc and his cat. There wasn't much she could do for the moment, but she still wanted to be useful. Her growling stomach reminded her it was well past lunch time, so she headed inside the house to make some sandwiches. When she made it to the kitchen and opened the fridge her mind went blank, staring at their limited lunch choices. They had grape jam, fruit cups, and a couple cans of pop. Looking further, she saw some lunch meat which was sadly a week past its expiration date. She grabbed the jar of jam with a despondent sigh and crossed to the pantry to find the peanut butter and a loaf of bread. Did billionaires eat PB and J sandwiches? Carly had no clue, but she was about to find out.

# 6

Luc wasn't sure how long he sat with Descartes, stroking the cat's soft white fur. Seeing Angeline's cat so ill had hit him harder than he imagined it would. Now he realized losing him would be like losing her all over again, and he couldn't bear the thought of that. Seeing Carly return with lunch gave him a welcome distraction.

"I hope you like peanut butter and jelly….cuz that's all we have."

He chuckled softly while taking a sandwich and a can of orange pop, for the first time noticing how cute she looked, wearing an oversized animal rescue t-shirt hanging loosely off one shoulder, cut off capris, and her blonde hair pulled up into a messy bun. He was so used to seeing her in scrubs with the Mulligan Animal Clinic logo on it. Her casual look was a nice change. "Peanut butter and jelly is just fine. It's what my mother used to make me for lunch all the time."

Her eyes widened. "Really?"

"Yes, believe it or not, I had a fairly normal childhood. When my parents divorced, my brother and I lived with our mother here in South Carolina, but we spent summers with our father in Paris."

She lifted an amused brow. "Oh, yes. Paris every summer sounds completely normal."

He nodded, feeling a grin form on his lips. Carly was brutally honest, but he enjoyed that facet of her personality. "Yes, I know how it sounds, but you might say, it was about as normal as a child in my family could have."

She shrugged while pulling up a chair across from him and taking a sandwich and drink for herself. "What's normal anyway?"

Luc grinned. "You may have a point there. I guess everyone has their own idea of what it should look like." He pulled the tab back on his can, enjoying the popping and fizzing sound immediately following. How long had it been since he'd opened a drink for himself? Over the years, since Angeline's passing, he'd fallen into the typical life of a billionaire bachelor, absorbed in his work and planning for the next business meeting. He'd grown accustomed to servers already having drinks poured into a glass and food prepared when they brought it to him and Luc had never thought much of it before. Now he liked the feeling of doing something for himself, even something so simple as opening his own can of soda. Sitting with Carly eating a simple lunch and sharing a casual conversation felt so natural.

Carly nodded before taking a bite of her sandwich and washing it down with some strawberry pop. "Life also has a way of flipping your routine on its end and changing everything, doesn't it?"

"I can't argue with that. So, what changed life for you, Carly?"

Her face turned serious as she finished her lunch and put the plate aside. "My brother's death. I blamed myself because I begged him to come home for my high school senior art exhibit. I thought if he hadn't been rushing to get home, he wouldn't have gotten in that wreck. I numbed my pain with unhealthy relationships and alcohol for several years. Now I realize there was no point in placing blame on anyone, including myself. It won't bring him back." She let out a nervous laugh. "I'm sorry. I'm sure you don't want to hear my sob story."

Luc studied her face, seeing the vulnerability behind her usual mask of sarcasm and witty personality. He could tell from the tear gathering in the corner of one eye, she didn't tell people personal things about herself often. She kept it hidden just beneath the surface, like he tended to do. "There's no need to apologize. You were honest, and I admire that."

Her shoulders relaxed as she nodded. "So, now that I've been honest…" One of Carly's brows arched, silently indicating it was his turn.

"I suppose you're curious about my abandoned studio?"

She nodded. "It has come to mind a few times." She leaned forward, her eyes kind instead of demanding. "I can tell how passionate you are about art from looking at the walls of your mansion. They are covered with Monet. Tell me if I'm wrong, but I'm guessing painting used to be a big part of your life."

He nodded as his defenses fell away. Somehow, he found it easier to talk with Carly who was little more than a stranger to him. Why was that? Luc had difficulty even discussing things like this with his mother, yet now he wanted to talk about it, almost *needed* to or thought he might burst. "You're right," he started out. "I began painting regularly when I was ten. The summer after my parents divorced, I visited Musée Marmottan Monet with my father. The museum has the largest collection of Monet's works in the world."

Carly's eyes lit up at the mention of the museum. "That sounds amazing. I'd love to visit it someday. So, that's what inspired you to paint?"

"It is. Monet's technique of forgetting the actual object but translating them into shapes and colors astounds me. It's…hard to describe…" All of a sudden, he was transported to Paris—back to the beloved museum, struggling to think of an English word to describe it. "It's … *tout simplement magnifique*," he finally blurted out with a flourish of his arm.

Carly laughed, but he could tell from the spark of excitement in her blue eyes, she wasn't laughing at him. He could sense the same passion for art in her heart as he had. "I'm not completely sure what that means, but I'm sure it would be an amazing sight to witness so many of his paintings all together in one place."

He nodded. "Yes, he and his fellow impressionists were not very appreciated in his time. They barely made a profit off their paintings, but it excites me to see others passionate about their work in modern times."

"And by continuing their example, you're keeping their techniques alive."

He shook his head. "I'd never compare myself to Monet as some of the islanders like to. He was far more accomplished as an artist than I will ever be."

She grinned at him. "You just said 'ever be.' I hope that means you'll pick up a brush again in the near future?"

Luc sighed before turning his attention back to Descartes. "Perhaps. To be honest, every artist has his muse. For Monet, it was light. For me…well, over the years it became Angeline. I'm afraid my desire to paint died with her."

"I'm sorry. I know this must be painful for you to talk about."

He looked up at her, astonished how she'd managed to gently break down some of his walls without him realizing. "It is. It's why I've held it inside all these years, but you helped me realize something."

"What's that?"

"Years of holding the pain in only made it fester, but letting it out might be the first step in helping it heal. I guess what I'm trying to say is, thank you for making me talk."

Carly smiled. "I'm excellent at talking. I'd be happy to give additional lessons free of charge any time."

He laughed at her snarky reply, feeling his burdens lift even more. "I may have to take you up on that, sooner rather than later."

Luc returned to the mansion at around four in the afternoon to rest and prepare for his business trip. He didn't like the idea of leaving Descartes alone in a new place for two days, but he had confidence Kendall and Carly would take care of him. He was glad he'd decided to clear his schedule for the day. It would have been pointless to go to attend his business meetings with the cat so ill. He doubted he'd have been able to concentrate on anything. It was also refreshing to spend a day away from his usual routine. However, the emotional rollercoaster he'd been on that day left him exhausted. A nap before dinner sounded wonderful, but for some reason, Luc felt drawn in the opposite direction from his bedroom. Soon he stood in the east wing, outside a familiar door. After mustering enough courage to enter, he stopped to gaze at the portrait Carly had uncovered a couple weeks ago. It was comforting in a way, knowing Angeline was there, her loving hazel eyes staring back at him, instead of hidden behind a sheet.

"*Bonjour, mon amour*," he murmured, walking further into the room. "You never did like it to be dark in this room, did you?" He crossed to the drapes and tied them back, allowing some light in and giving him a clear view of the gardens. A few early spring perennials were beginning to peek through the soil. In a month or two, he knew the entire area would be bursting with colors.

After allowing himself a moment to take in Angeline's favorite view from the estate, he turned around to study the room. Besides her portrait, all the other pieces hanging on the wall were still covered in sheets. He shook his head in regret. She would have hated for his studio to look this way. It was time for a change.

One by one, he uncovered each painting, until a tall mound of sheets rested on the floor. He looked around with an approving nod before turning to his large easel in the center of the room, still covered. His hand rested on top of it for a moment before lifting it again. "One step at a time," he whispered. "One step at a time."

7

After lunchtime on Monday, Carly left Kendall to man the clinic and took Athena for an appointment with Melody at her mobile grooming station. The auburn-haired groomer knew her sister, Kendall, from camp years ago, but Carly had become fast friends with her after consulting on several patients in the last few months. Melody gave her a warm hug when she arrived and invited her in.

"It's so good to see you again. When you're not so busy, I'd really like to go have lunch with you and Kendall."

"I'd love to."

Melody watched as Carly took the Himalayan cat out of the carrier. "Who is this sweetheart?"

"This is Athena. She was actually a stray brought in by Annie. She's as sweet as can be, just severely matted from so many months out on the streets. Do you think there's anything you can do? Kendall and I thought of giving her a lion cut."

Her friend's eyes grew wide with horror. "Oh, I'm so glad you didn't! Always come to me before you even think of doing that."

Carly chuckled. "I will. I promise."

Melody put Athena up on the table and placed a little leash around the cat's neck to keep her from going anywhere. She looked her over well, before trying to untangle some of the mats with her fingers first, explaining her technique as she went. After a few minutes, she retrieved a bottle of detangler and a comb from a nearby drawer. "Now, patience is the key with this next step. If she starts to get matted again after this, you'll want to apply an oil-based detangler like this and use a metal comb. Use short quick strokes like this," she explained while demonstrating. "Now never, I repeat *never*, try to cut the mats off."

Carly nodded and continued to watch Melody as she groomed Athena, little by little, revealing her beautiful gray coat. It took almost an hour, but the cat was enjoying the attention so much, she purred, drooled and eventually laid down on the table and almost fell asleep, causing them both to laugh.

"Well, she really is a sweetheart, isn't she?" Melody commented as she finished and took the leash off the cat's neck. "I've never had a cat be so cooperative."

"Yes, she adores attention. That's for sure."

"Well, I'd take her if I had the room. She's such a pretty and loving little girl. I'll be praying she finds a good home."

Carly smiled while placing Athena back in her carrier. "Thanks so much. I really appreciate your help. Are you sure you won't take any money?"

Melody shook her head. "No, you don't owe me a cent. You all are always so helpful to consult with when I have medical questions about pets, I'm happy to barter and help each other out when needed."

Carly thanked her friend again before leaving with Athena. After returning to the clinic, she greeted Kendall who was working at her desk and let Athena out of her carrier.

Her sister smiled and petted Athena as she rubbed against her leg. "Hello, little beauty. Don't you look pretty with all your mats detangled?"

"Melody did a beautiful job, didn't she?"

Kendall nodded. "Yes. She's a miracle worker." She looked up at Carly after Athena wandered away to rub against a table leg. "I just have a few more things to do on the computer. Would you mind checking on Descartes and giving him a midday meal? He seems to eat better when I feed him small amounts, so I thought feeding him three times a day might be beneficial."

"Sure." Carly went through the dividing door and Athena followed her, rubbing against her legs and almost making her trip a few times. When they reached the boarding cages, the Angora cat was rubbing up against the bars, meowing. Kendall had removed his IV the night before, after his condition had improved. He'd grown used to them too, no longer hissing and growling at them when they came into the RV.

"Well, good afternoon, boy. Glad to see you have so much energy." She opened a can of food and put some into his bowl before reaching to unlock the cage. He snuck right past her hand through the narrow opening and leapt onto the floor. "You little sneak!" She watched him scamper across the floor, coming face to face with Athena. At first, they just stared at each other. Then Descartes' ears flattened against his head, hissing and growling. Athena paused for a few seconds, but then she inched forward, rubbing up against the Angora cat before rolling onto her back with her gray belly in the air.

Descartes studied her for a while, moving into a sitting position. His ears perked back up as Athena continued laying in a submissive position and began to purr. The male cat gave her a curious sniff before stalking away with an arrogant flip of his tail.

Carly laughed so hard tears flowed down her cheeks. "Looks like Athena used her secret weapon against you, Descartes…kindness!"

She put his food and a small bowl of water on the floor close to him, curious what would happen. His eyes darted around suspiciously to make sure Athena wasn't close by before chowing down.

"Bravo, Descartes!" Watching him eat so well was an encouraging sight.

Kendall opened the door and took a double take when she saw the Angora cat out of his cage. "Wow, is that the same cat? I've never seen him eat that well."

Carly nodded. "I think he didn't want Athena to get it. I didn't let him out here. He did that all on his own and somehow Athena had a positive effect on him."

"Yes, I can see that. I think we should leave them out together in this back area for the rest of the day and maybe even bring them into the house together tonight to see what happens."

She grinned after hearing her sister's idea. "I see where you're going with this. I think it just might work."

Luc arrived back on Elnora Tuesday afternoon, right on schedule. He wanted to rest after his trip, but instead asked his chauffeur to take him to Captain's Walk on Merriweather where Carly and Kendall parked their RV. He opted for the Rolls-Royce instead of the limo to be more inconspicuous than the last time. However, the luxury car still stuck out like a sore thumb as his driver parked by the mobile clinic. He ignored a few islanders gawking while walking up to knock on the door.

Carly opened the door with a wide grin. "Hey stranger, how was your trip?"

Her happy mood was contagious, drawing a smile from his lips as well. "Long, but I'm glad to be home. How is Descartes?"

She opened the door a little wider and motioned with her free arm. "Come in and see for yourself."

He followed her up the stairs and through a small waiting

area to the door leading to the exam room and boarding area. When they entered, his eyes grew wide with surprise, seeing Descartes playing with a Himalayan cat. He startled when the door made a noise and hid underneath the exam table. Luc turned to Carly. "He's actually been playing with another cat?"

She nodded. "Yes, I was shocked when I first saw it, too. It took about half the day on Monday, but Athena was determined for him to like her. By the evening, they were inseparable."

Luc shook his head in disbelief while sitting in a foldable chair in the corner of the room. "It's all right, Descartes," he called. "You can come out and play with your friend. I won't bother you."

It took the cat a minute or two to come out. He gave Luc an apprehensive glance before walking up to Athena and rubbing against her. Soon, they were romping around again, chasing and pouncing on each other.

He laughed out loud watching them. "Wow, it's a total transformation! Are you sure this is my cat?"

Kendall chuckled as she put away a few supplies. "Yes, Mr. Belshaw. He's still your cat. As you can see, he's feeling more like himself."

"More like himself? I've never seen Descartes play, or have this much energy, as long as I've known him anyway."

Carly grinned from across the room. "I wanted to talk with you about that if you have time. Would you like to take a short walk down to the ferry slip?"

Luc nodded, his mouth hurting from smiling so much. "Sure, a walk sounds wonderful."

He followed her outside, curiosity getting the better of him. They walked for a while, enjoying the views of Reginald Square and the ocean as they came closer to the slip. Carly's blonde curls distracted him as they blew in the sea breeze. "So, what was it you wanted to talk to me about? I hope nothing is wrong with Descartes."

She shook her head. "No, he has a clean bill of health now and is eating and drinking normally."

He released a deep sigh of relief. "That's good to hear. As I told you before, I haven't been much of a cat person in the past, but Descartes meant so much to Angeline. I want to make sure he's as happy and healthy as possible."

"Yes, I can see that now. Which is why Kendall and I wanted to mention something we think will help keep him that way."

"What's that?"

"A therapy cat." Carly led him to a stone bench and they sat together, watching the ferry leaving to transport people to the mainland. "Athena is a stray we've been fostering and we've discovered that she's been able to help Descartes. Whenever she's around, he's been eating and drinking normally. He's also been playful, as you saw in the clinic."

He rubbed his chin thoughtfully. "A therapy cat, huh? I wondered what caused such a dramatic change in him."

"Yeah, we were surprised by that, too. I think Descartes was lonely."

Luc studied Carly's expectant blue eyes, finally realizing what the conversation was about. "Are you asking me to adopt Athena?"

Carly swallowed hard and fidgeted with her necklace. "Only on a trial basis. If it doesn't work out, you can bring her right back."

Luc shook his head, not believing what he was hearing. "I'm sorry, but I can barely handle one cat in my life as it is. Plus, I'm away all the time. Doesn't Athena deserve an owner who can spend time with her?"

"You have Mrs. Potter for that, right? Plus, if Descartes and Athena have each other, they won't be starved for attention." He started to make up another excuse, but she interrupted, the desperation in her eyes making him stop. "Please, just hear me out. Athena is healthy with all her shots. She's also litterboxtrained and doesn't scratch furniture as long as she has her scratching post. To top it all off, she has the sweetest personality. Even non-cat lovers like yourself would fall in love with her quickly."

He chuckled softly, avoiding her pleading gaze. "Why do I feel like I've just been given a sales pitch by a traveling salesperson?"

"Sorry, I'm not usually so pushy. I just want Athena to find a good home and for Descartes to be happy. Can you blame me?"

"No, I suppose not." Luc paused, gazing at the ocean view while thinking about what she asked. With all the decisions coming up in his life, it was difficult to consider taking on another responsibility. "Can I think about it for a few days?" he finally asked.

"Of course, you can. I know you'd need time to prepare for a new cat in the house, if you decide to take her."

The walk back to the clinic seemed to take a lifetime. Carly was silent and Luc was lost in his own thoughts, too. He did want the best for Descartes, but it was a big decision to adopt another pet, especially for someone who wasn't really a cat person in the first place. He would take his cat home, observe his behavior for a few days, and think about what Carly suggested.

"Oh, rich people!" Carly grumbled with a stomp of her foot as the fancy luxury car pulled away with Luc and Descartes inside. "He could help his cat and another at the same time, but he just doesn't want to."

Kendall stopped putting supplies away for a moment to look at her. "Just because he didn't answer the way we hoped, doesn't mean he doesn't care. You told me yourself, he raises money for animal shelters in his wife's name, didn't you?"

Carly puffed air and crossed her arms. "Yes, I did."

"And didn't he say he would think about it?"

Carly nodded. "All right. I guess you have some valid points. It just seemed like such a perfect solution."

Kendall gave her a knowing smile, before leaning down to pick up Athena and stroke her soft fur. "Yes, it did, but we'll find another one if it doesn't work out." Carly nodded in agreement before her sister went on. "Now, would you help me clean up? I'd like to get started on dinner early tonight. I have a lot of invoices to enter on my computer."

"Of course," Carly agreed while folding up the chair Luc had been sitting on. "Sorry for being such a grump."

"I don't think you're being a grump. You're just passionate about trying to find solutions. God will work everything out. We'll just have to pray for wisdom for what to do next."

Carly's shoulders started to relax after her sister's reassuring words and within about ten minutes, they were on their way home. She stayed quiet most of the way, thinking over her sister's words. It was true that God worked things out. When they first came to Merriweather, she had been so bitter about her brother's death, it led to problems she couldn't see her way out of, but He showed the way, once she was willing to see it. She had no doubts He would do it again.

When they reached the house, Carly went to work feeding Zoe and Athena while Kendall prepared a simple meal for dinner. She came into their small eat-in kitchen and started setting the table when someone knocked on the door.

Kendall finished flipping a grilled cheese sandwich and glanced at the clock. "Were you expecting anyone to come by tonight?"

"No, I don't think so." Carly headed toward the door and opened it without releasing the chain, an old habit from living in the city. Peering out, she saw a pair of familiar blue eyes staring back at her. "Luc?"

His charming smile made her heart race. "I'm sorry. I came at a bad time, didn't I?"

"No, it's fine, really. Just hold on a sec." Carly closed the door enough to release the chain, before opening it all the way to let him in. She looked down, noticing the cat carrier in his hand as he stepped over the threshold. "Is something wrong with Descartes?"

He shook his head as she closed the door behind him. "No... well. Actually...yes. In a way something is wrong. You see, Descartes was miserable after we got into the car, yowling and making a fuss. I've never seen him act quite that way before. I think he missed Athena."

On cue, the cat trotted into the room, straight to the cat carrier. Both cats started purring right away and butting their heads against the bars.

Carly chuckled watching them. "Yeah, it seems they both missed each other."

"Anyway," Luc continued. "I decided I would like to give Athena a chance to live in the mansion. I figured, what could it hurt?"

Before Carly realized it, she'd squealed and wrapped him in a tight hug. "Thank you! I'm sure you're going to love Athena. She is so sweet, loving and..." She paused, craning her neck to look up at Luc, whose eyes darted around, avoiding her eyes. Carly released him and stepped back. "Sorry, I get overly excited and impulsive sometimes."

"That's fine," he assured, letting an apprehensive laugh escape his lips. "Really, think nothing of it. Anyway, I'd like to take both cats home with me tonight, if that's all right with you both."

"Sure, that would be great!" Carly said a little more enthusiastically than she meant to. It was hard to control her emotions after such wonderful news.

"Who is it?" her sister called from the kitchen.

"It's Mr. Belshaw."

"Oh good. Why don't you invite him to stay for dinner?"

Carly turned back to Luc, feeling heat rising to her cheeks at the thought of him staying any longer. "Would you like to stay? We're having grilled cheese sandwiches and tomato soup."

He smiled again, causing her heart to pound. "That sounds perfect."

# 8

After the initial awkward hug from Carly, Luc's meal with the Mulligans was a pleasant experience. In fact, it was one of the best evenings he'd had in a long time. Both sisters were easy to talk to and didn't swoon over him like most women did when they found out about his wealthy family. They were curious about his life and asked plenty of questions about his family's business in Paris. When they were finished eating, Kendall started putting leftovers away and then excused herself to check her email.

Luc followed Carly into the living room and sat on the sofa next to her. They watched a game show in awkward silence for a minute before he broke the ice. "Your sister keeps busy, doesn't she? Every time I see her, she always seems to be on a mission."

Carly shrugged. "We try to split the responsibilities, being roommates and all. It was her turn to make dinner and clean up. Tomorrow it will be mine. But she tends to keep busy no matter what. She has a type A personality and like things to be a certain way. I, on the other hand, am type B and like things a bit more spontaneous."

He arched an amused eyebrow. "I would guess that about you."

Carly grinned at his statement and let out a sigh before relaxing against the couch cushions. "Anyway, tonight Kendall has other reasons for checking her email than our animal clinic business. Her boyfriend is on tour in the Middle East. Since there's an eight-hour time difference, they have a hard time catching each other during the day on video chat, so they email and write letters a lot. He probably wrote her something while we were working. Now she'll respond so he can read it first thing when he wakes up in the morning. They are so lovey dovey it almost nauseates me sometimes."

He chuckled at her playful eye roll. "That's nice they keep in touch. Is he from New England like the both of you?"

"No, he's a local on Merriweather. His name is Tyler Banner. Have you heard of him or his sister, Tiffany?"

He thought for a few moments and then nodded. "Yes, I have. I didn't grow up here on the Islands, like them, but I'm acquainted with them. Tiffany and her husband came to one of the art exhibits I used to host. They bought one of my pieces called, 'Sunset at Pirate's Cove', I believe."

Carly's eyes widened at the mention of the painting. "That is one of yours? I can't stop admiring it every time I go over to Tiff's house!"

"Yes, one of my favorites, actually." His stomach tangled into knots, but he managed to cover up his discomfort with a fake smile. Carly always managed to tie the conversation back to his art. While it was nice of her to compliment his work, it was a part of his past—a part he preferred not to speak of yet. It was like he was a child again, refusing to allow his mother to remove a bandage from a healing scrape on his knee. They both knew it needed to be removed to allow the wound to properly heal, but he continued to resist for most of the day, fearing the raw pain would return with a vengeance.

"Are you all right?" she asked after a long silence between them.

He nodded and stood to stretch. "I'm fine. I think some fresh air might do me some good though. Would you like to go outside?"

She agreed and they checked on the cats who had sprawled out on the floor beside each other, content as could be with Zoe watching them with curious eyes. Then they headed out the back door. Carly breathed in the salty air as they walked down the beach to the edge of the water, watching the remnants of the sunset fade from the sky. "This is my favorite part of living on the Islands...right here."

He watched with her as the moon rose higher in the night sky. "I agree. When I lived with my mother on Hilton Head, we enjoyed sitting outside at night. Sometimes on warm nights I'd fall asleep in a hammock, listening to the waves."

Carly smiled at him. "That sounds wonderful."

"Yeah, it was. However, when I went to Paris in the summer, I had a hard time falling asleep when the sounds of the ocean were replaced by the sounds of the city."

"I imagine it would be difficult. I had the opposite problem when we first moved here. Kendall teased me I should find a recording of car sounds, ambulances, and honking horns to fall asleep to."

He chuckled while watching the stars begin to appear. "Did you try to find one?"

"No, I got used to the quiet after a while. Now the sound is like a welcome friend." She rubbed her arms while talking.

"Are you cold?"

"A little. I might go in and find a sweater."

"Here, allow me." He removed his blazer and placed it over her shoulders. "Is that better?"

She snuggled into the garment and nodded. "Yes. Thank you." Carly studied his face in the dim glow from the moon and then took his hand. "Come on. I want to show you something."

Luc followed, overwhelmed by the feeling of Carly's palm in his as she led him to a set of chairs. She motioned for him to sit before taking the chair next to him. "I like to come out here at night. No matter what happens during the day, I know I can come out to our backyard and let the sound of the waves soothe my mind." She kicked off her flip flops and lounged in the oversized chair, closing her eyes. He followed suit, but his shoulders remained tense. She peeked over at him through one eyelid. "Come on! You need to learn how to relax. Take off your shoes and let your toes wiggle in the sand."

"You want me to do what?"

She scoffed and gave him a playful swat on the arm. "You heard me. Now, just try it. I promise, it's very therapeutic. Also, I find if you go barefoot in the sand often, you'll never have to use a pumice stone."

He chuckled at her statement, but did what she asked, surprised to discover the sand still held some warmth from the day. He closed his eyes and felt his body relax. "You're right, this is relaxing. It's a nice change from the hustle and bustle of New York the past few days."

He heard the creak of Carly's chair as she shifted to face him. "Do you enjoy traveling all the time?"

He shrugged, keeping his eyes closed. "I guess I do, in a way. It's nice to have a change of scenery and it has become my normal these days, I suppose. It used to be exciting to travel to new places all the time." Luc's memories drifted where he didn't wish them to go, but he decided to speak them out loud anyway. For some odd reason, he was beginning to trust Carly, even though they'd only known each other for a few weeks. He didn't have to be guarded around her. "When I traveled with Angeline...even on business trips...she'd make sure I squeezed in some time to go sightseeing and paint. It's why I have pieces from all over the world. Now, when I travel, it's just a blur of long flights, hotels, and meetings."

"Sounds like you're well past due for some R&R. Will you promise me something?"

He opened his eyes and turned toward her, distracted for a moment by the glow of the moonlight highlighting the curves of her face. "What's that?"

"Next time you go on a business trip, take some time for yourself. Even if it's only an hour. Use me for an excuse if you have to and snap a few pictures to show me when you come back. I've never been out of the US, except a trip to Cancun for spring break in college a few years back."

A grin tingled on his lips. "All right. I'll agree to that, but only if you promise to save up for your own trip abroad someday in the near future. There are so many wonderful things to see, and I don't want you to miss out either."

She studied him for a moment with a furrowed brow. Had he rendered the girl who always had something to say speechless? When he could take the silence no longer, she finally responded. "I wouldn't even know where to start. There's so many places I'd like to go, but I've never been able to save enough to go."

"You will," he encouraged. "Just make it a goal. I have connections in the travel industry who could find some amazing discounts for your trip."

She chuckled. "Guess it's good to have friends in high places. Well, you convinced me. I'll start saving up." She sat up and reached to shake his hand. "It's a deal, Mr. Belshaw."

The following morning when Luc's alarm went off at six o'clock, he was quick to turn it off and press the button to close his room darkening shades. He'd purposely not scheduled any meetings or conference calls until the afternoon because of his trip but had forgotten to change the settings on his alarm the night before. He'd spent longer at the Mulligans' house than he intended, not arriving back at the mansion until well after eleven. By the time he helped Descartes and Athena settle in to their new living arrangements, it was past midnight. The late bedtime coupled with jetlag from his trip made him want to go into hibernation mode.

He'd barely managed to fall back asleep when the intercom beeped. He fumbled for the button in the dark and mashed it after several failed attempts. "What is it?" he slurred, opening one eye to see it came from Descartes room.

Mrs. Potter's voice came through the speaker a little too loudly, causing him to wince. "I apologize for disturbing you, Mr. Belshaw, but there appears to be a new cat in Descartes' room. I have no clue how she got in here. Maybe a stray from outside snuck in?"

Luc grinned in spite of his groggy state of mind. "It's all right. She's Descartes' therapy cat."

"Therapy cat? I've never heard of something like that."

He chuckled, hearing the confusion and mild distress in the voice of his ultra-organized secretary. "I'll explain later. For now, could you please give her some of Descartes' food in one of his extra bowls?"

"Yes, sir. I can do that."

"Good. Also, can you please hold any calls and my breakfast until eight?"

Mrs. Potter agreed, although sounding a little perplexed. Being a morning person, it was almost unheard of for Luc to sleep in, unless he was under the weather. However, he flopped onto his stomach and hugged his pillow, hoping just once the household would get along without him for a few hours.

When his alarm went off again at eight, Luc opened his automatic curtains, ready to begin the day. After breakfast, he headed down to check on the cats. When he opened the door, Athena was the first to greet him, curling around his legs and meowing for attention. He bent down to pet her. *"Bonjour, doux petite mademoiselle."* Athena responded by rubbing against his foot and dissolving into a furry, purring puddle on the ground. He chuckled while petting her a little longer. "You love attention, don't you?" After she seemed content, he stood to look for Descartes who'd dashed away to hide when he walked in. A short scan of the room revealed he had retreated to the bottom level of his cat condo. Luc's heart sank as he tried to coax him out. Had the cat fallen back into old habits? He seemed so happy at the Mulligans' house.

Luc decided to try again tomorrow and headed down the hallway to his studio. It was easier to enter each time and seeing Angeline's portrait first thing helped somehow. He opened the drapes again, allowing light to flood through the large bay window before relaxing onto the divan. The room used to be his favorite refuge and he hoped it could be that again someday, if he took it one step at a time. It was amazing to think only weeks ago, he'd been avoiding the room like the plague, but somehow Carly entering it changed that. Her presence in his life changed a lot of things in such a short amount of time. Luc wanted to see her again, sooner rather than later, but needed to think of a creative way to make it happen.

## 9

The next week raced by as Kendall and Carly were swamped with appointments and busy preparing pamphlets to pass out for the Sweethearts Festival taking place that weekend on Elnora. They'd reserved a spot at the park to give tours of the mobile clinic and partnered with a local animal shelter on the mainland, who brought some of their animals available for adoption. It was a great way to promote the new clinic and help some animals in need of homes, but preparing for it all took a lot of planning.

She was thankful to be busy though because it took her mind off of Athena. Carly hadn't realized how attached she'd become to the little cat until Luc took Athena to live at the mansion. It felt strange no longer having her weaving between her legs and almost tripping her every morning when it was time to be fed. However, she was grateful Luc had offered to give her a home, at least temporarily. They barely had enough space for Zoe in their little beach house, and the litter box took up a large section of the bathroom, so it was a much better arrangement for all involved. Still, she wanted to go visit Athena soon to see how she was acclimating to her new home. Plus, it would give her a valid excuse to see the cat's handsome billionaire foster parent.

Carly had tried to keep Luc out of her thoughts, and when she couldn't manage not to, she tried to focus on the friendship they were forming instead of the obvious attraction between them. She always fell for guys too fast. It was like an addiction, and she was determined to not let it happen with Luc. Sure, he was tall, handsome, and artistic, but she barely knew him. She'd never met his family, and his wealth concerned her. She was just a normal twenty something girl from Boston. Before moving to Merriweather with Kendall, she'd lived in a tiny apartment off campus with her roommate, Marie. They'd barely made enough money working part-time jobs to support themselves while in college.

Now, going into business with her sister, she was a little better off. Their list of clients was growing, but they still had to live on a tight budget. Luc wouldn't have any clue what it felt like to live like that and she couldn't imagine growing up wealthy. Would that difference put a wedge between them in the future? That question and dozens more had snuck up on her during the week, but she tried her hardest to banish them from her thoughts. It was likely Luc wasn't attracted to her at all anyway. He was a widower who probably wasn't ready to date anytime soon. It was clear Carly needed to stop creating problems out of thin air. The fact was, they wouldn't be compatible, so there was no point worrying about it in the first place.

Before Carly knew it, the morning of the Sweethearts Festival on Elnora had arrived. She woke up early and started helping Kendall load everything into the RV, including some posters she'd made by hand.

"Those are stunning," her sister said as she found a safe place to store the signs. "Who needs to pay for a printer to make our signs when I have a talented sister like you?"

"Thanks, sis." She smiled and noticed her sister's puffy eyes. "Is everything all right?"

Kendall nodded. "I'm fine. Just missing Tyler this morning. You know, it's our first Valentine's Day as a couple, and we're spending it apart." She paused to wipe her eyes and forced a smile. "I knew what I was getting into, with him being away for so long. It's just tough sometimes, you know?"

She hugged her sister. "Yeah, I can imagine. How about we have a special girls' night tonight? We'll order something to go from Granny's and take it home. We can watch a few of those tear-jerker movies you love so much. Then we can eat some of that chocolate chip cookie dough ice cream we have been saving."

Kendall nodded against her. "That sounds perfect."

"Good, it's a sister date then. I'm sorry, I didn't think of how you must be feeling. I've been so distracted lately."

Her sister giggled and pulled back, wiping a few more tears. "Distracted by The Elnora Monet?"

Carly scoffed and turned away to hide her blushing cheeks from Kendall. "No, I hardly thought of him at all," she lied while straightening a few things in the RV.

The sound of a vehicle coming down their gravel driveway caught her attention and saved her from any further teasing. "Who is that?"

"Looks like a flower delivery van."

Carly followed Kendall down the driveway past the RV. It wasn't common to see a flower delivery service on the Islands, especially at such an early hour, but there it was.

"I have a delivery for a Kendall Mulligan. Does she live at this residence?" the man asked.

"That's me," Kendall said, stepping forward as he handed her a vase with two dozen red roses paired with baby's breath. It also came with a card and box of chocolates. Her sister thanked the delivery guy and turned to her with more tears as he drove away. "It's from Tyler. How sweet is that? I'm going to go put these inside. I'll be back out in a few minutes."

Carly watched with a smile as her sister hurried inside with her Valentine's surprise. "Way to go, Tyler," she whispered to herself. "You've got my approval." It was wonderful to see her sister so happy. Yet, it made her heart ache a little. It would be Carly's first Valentine's Day alone in a long time. She always found herself some kind of date to celebrate the occasion, but not this year. She was done focusing on meaningless, unhealthy relationships. She wanted someone who was ready to make a long-term commitment, like her sister had found. If it meant waiting for as long as Kendall had, so be it.

By the time Carly had the RV ready to go, her sister returned, dabbing at her eyes with a tissue but sporting a mile-wide smile. "I called Tiff. He had everything set up in advance."

"Couldn't leave it a mystery, could you?"

Kendall shook her head. "Nope. You know me. I had to meddle."

They chuckled together while hopping into the mobile clinic and heading for Elnora. By the time they arrived at the park, it was almost eight and most of the other booths were set up. They parked in their reserved spot and met up with the owner of the animal shelter who was sharing the space with them.

After they were set up, Carly spent some time looking at the animals up for adoption. A small dog pen was placed in the grass, allowing three golden Labrador Retriever puppies to romp around and play. There were also three adult dogs in separate crates, and about half a dozen cats and kittens. She petted the puppies first and laughed as they wrestled with each other. They were so fluffy, adorable, and playful, Carly had no doubt they would find loving homes by the end of the day. After petting the puppies, she asked Tammy, the owner, if she could help.

"Sure, I'd love help." Tammy smiled and handed her a stack

of laminated cards and wooden clips. "Would you mind clipping these information cards on the crates?"

"Sure." Carly went around doing as she said, looking up periodically to ask her what card belonged to which animal. She talked to each animal in a soothing voice. When she moved on to the last dog crate, she looked down at the card and smiled. "You must be Charlie." The senior beagle let out a funny howl and wagged his tail so rapidly, his entire body wiggled. "Well, aren't you a sweetheart?"

"Yes, he is," Tammy agreed, coming up beside her. "I'm hoping today will be Charlie's lucky day to find a forever home. It's been two years since he first came to our shelter."

Carly's eyes widened. "Two years?"

"Yeah, unfortunately, it's harder to find owners for the senior animals."

She frowned, reaching through the crate to pat Charlie's head. "Poor boy. I'd take you myself if we had a fenced in yard."

Tammy nodded. "Yes, that's part of the problem with beagles. Whoever adopts him will need one because his nose persuades him to wander away. I've lowered his adoption fee to half price to encourage people to give him a chance. Hopefully it will work."

"Yeah, I hope so, too."

After helping Tammy, the festival started and Carly returned to the table they'd set up in front of the RV. She and Kendall spent the morning handing out pamphlets about the clinic and took turns giving tours. By lunchtime, they were both worn out, but happy to have met so many potential customers. Carly was also happy to see some of the animals had been adopted. All the puppies were gone as she predicted, along with several of the cats, kittens, and one dog. However, poor Charlie was still there, wagging his tail and howling at each person who passed by.

"I don't know about you, but I'm famished," Kendall said from beside her.

Carly tore her gaze from the beagle and nodded. "Yeah, me too. Do you want me to head over to Beth's food truck and buy an order of her shrimp tacos?"

"That sounds amazing."

"All right. I'll be back soon." She headed across the park to the Comfort Cuisine and blinked hard, balking at the long line. Beth would run out of food before she reached the front of it. However, as she looked around at some booths nearby serving food, she decided all the lines looked equally long if not worse. Even if her friend had run out of shrimp, she could order something else. All the food she offered was delicious anyway. Carly took her place in line and a few people filed in behind her. It was about twenty minutes before she reached the front of the line to make her order.

Beth's face lit up when she saw her. "Carly! I was wondering if I'd see you and Kendall here today."

She smiled, relieved to see her friend's familiar face. Beth was always so pleasant and easy to talk to. "Yeah, our RV is set up across the way. We've been so busy. This is the first chance I've had to get away."

"I bet you're half starved. What can I get for you?"

"Two orders of shrimp tacos…if you have any left, and two pink lemonades, please."

Beth grinned. "Yep, I've still got some. Your order will be up soon."

Carly thanked her and stood off to the side while her friend took some more orders. Her attention drifted to all the happy couples walking around the festival, holding hands, dancing, and playing games at the booths. She'd been busy all day, keeping the fact she was alone far from her thoughts, but now the gloomy feeling snuck up on her again.

Beth's voice cut through her thoughts as she greeted another customer. "Sorry for the long wait, Mr. Belshaw. What can I get for you today?"

Carly's eyes flew to the man as he made his order. He was wearing jeans and a casual polo shirt today, throwing her completely off. Yet, there was Luc, standing a few feet away from her.

She stood speechless as he finished making his order. He smiled and walked over to stand beside her. "Good afternoon, Carly."

"Hi," she managed with a nervous giggle. "How long were you lurking behind me?"

Luc ran his fingers through his dark hair with a boyish grin. "I wasn't exactly *lurking*, but I did happen to notice it was you in front of me a few minutes ago. It's been kind of nice blending in with the crowd. I even took my own car today, believe it or not. Beth's been one of the first to recognize me so far."

Carly realized her mouth was hanging open and closed it before speaking again. "How do you know Beth?"

"Oh, she catered for one of my charity events recently. Her food is the best."

"Yeah, it is."

A second later, Beth opened the window to hand Carly and Luc their orders. "Thanks so much. Have fun at the festival."

Carly thanked her and walked away, carrying her food with Luc hurrying to catch up. "So, how's everything going?"

"Good. We've been so busy this week, plus preparing for the festival. I've hardly had time to breathe. How are Descartes and Athena?"

Luc took a sip from his straw before answering. "They're excellent, actually. I've never seen Descartes so happy and Athena is sweet as can be. She always wants attention and has started following me around the mansion. Descartes tags along sometimes, but he still doesn't want to be petted."

"Hopefully that will change with a little time."

Luc nodded. "Yeah, I don't want to rush him. He's been eating and drinking though, so that's an improvement."

"I'm happy to hear it." Carly realized they were almost back to where the clinic was parked and gulped when Kendall spotted them.

Her sister waved them over. "It's nice to see you, Mr. Belshaw. Please, come join us. We have plenty of room at the table."

"Sure, I'd love to. Thank you for the invitation."

"I'll go find another folding chair," Carly responded before escaping into the RV. While looking for the chair, she struggled to slow her pounding heart. Why did he have to show up? She'd finally managed to banish him from her thoughts and now he was here, torturing her with his presence.

When Carly came back out, she placed the chair at the table for Luc and sat at the opposite side of the table, putting as much distance between her and Luc as possible. Tammy soon joined them with a lunch she'd packed for herself. Everyone carried on with small talk, but Carly couldn't keep track of what they were talking about. She came out of her fog when Luc started asking Tammy about the animals up for adoption.

"We're doing well today," Tammy told him. "But unfortunately, it's been difficult to find people to adopt the older animals."

Luc's eyes lit up. "I'll pay for all the adoption fees for anyone who wants to take home a pet today. Would that help?"

Tammy smiled at him. "Thank you so much. That's very generous. However, I think most people have gone over to the carnival games now or dancing. We would need something to attract them back over here."

"That is a dilemma." Luc rubbed his chin, before scooting his chair out to stand. "I have an idea. My home isn't that far away. I'll be back in twenty minutes. Carly, in the meantime, is there any way you could make a new sign?"

She nodded. "I could use the back of one I've already made. I've got some permanent markers in the RV."

"That will do just fine."

She stared at him, puzzled. "What do you want it to say?"

"Free Sweetheart Sketches by The Elnora Monet." He started to leave, before turning back to add, "Make sure you say all donations will go to the animal shelter. If the rest of you could start spreading the word, that would be great."

He rushed off before any of them had a chance to respond. Carly turned to her sister with a wide grin. "Well, I've never seen him so animated."

Kendall giggled. "Neither have I, but I think his plan will definitely draw attention."

## 10

Luc was halfway home before second guessing his spontaneous decision. He hadn't been able to paint, not to mention sketch, in two years, yet he'd just volunteered to sketch portraits for the Sweethearts Festival? There was no telling how many people would be in line for something free. Also, did he really want to set this precedence? He'd grown so used to being a recluse, besides hosting private charity events having nothing to do with art. Now would people be expecting him to start hosting public exhibits again?

He started looking for a place to turn his convertible around. Maybe if he returned to the festival in time, he could stop Carly from making the poster and the others from spreading the word about his offer. However, in the end he couldn't make himself do it. Luc had never been a man to go back on his word, and he wasn't about to start now.

When Luc arrived at the mansion, he hurried to his studio to grab a few unused sketchpads and drawing pencils on the shelf before heading back out the way he came. Athena sat by her door with a confused look on her face. "Sorry, *petite mademoiselle*! I'll be back tonight." He received odd looks from

Mrs. Potter, the butler, and his security guard on the way out, but decided to explain later. At the moment, returning to the festival was his top priority.

When he arrived, Carly had the poster ready and there were already a few couples lined up for portraits. Luc took a deep breath before sitting at the table and having the first couple pose for the portrait. At first the pencil felt foreign in his hand. He drew a few lines before his hand started to shake. The pencil dropped on the ground and rolled under the table.

Carly retrieved the pencil and placed it back in his hand. She didn't speak, but her calming gaze reassured him he could do it.

He thanked her and tried again, slowly at first. After the first few strokes, the technique came back to him and shapes and shadows took shape on the page. Before Luc knew it, he had signed one portrait and had moved onto the next. It felt like the artist side of his personality had been asleep for a long time, and now it was waking back up.

Carly watched Luc in amazement as he completed portrait after portrait. She'd never seen him look more free and alive. The concentration on his face and movement of his eyebrows as he made the strokes on the paper were fascinating. The pencil seemed like an extension of his hand. She had loved art since childhood, but had never possessed the confidence to use her talent in public like Luc was doing, yet she felt a connection to him in that moment. Even though he had repressed it for two years, the same hunger to create lived in both of their hearts.

As Luc drew the portraits, there was plenty of action happening by the pet adoption station, too. Carly's heart sang as several people filled out paperwork to adopt dogs and cats. When the crowd started to thin out, she saw a middle-aged couple looking at Charlie the beagle. Tammy let him out of the crate to meet the couple and Carly held her breath. She closed her eyes and said a prayer before opening them again.

"I used to have a dog like this when I was a kid." The man rubbed Charlie's belly and looked up at his wife. "What do you think?"

His wife agreed and Carly could barely contain herself. After the papers were signed, they sat for Luc's last portrait for the day with Charlie sitting on their laps, happy as could be. Carly wished she could have a copy of the portrait, but at least she had the memory in her mind. Luc's generosity had helped so many animals find their forever home that day. It made her look at him in a different light. Maybe they weren't as incompatible as she thought.

When the last couple left, Luc put his pencil down and stretched his fingers before lounging back in his chair. "Talk about an artistic marathon," he said with a chuckle.

Carly grinned and sat next to him, no longer feeling awkward like earlier in the day. "Thank you for everything you did today."

He shrugged. "Oh, it wasn't much."

"Yes, it was. Your idea made all the difference in those animals finding homes. Thank you."

"You're welcome." Luc sighed with a happy grin on his face. "You know, I never thought I'd be able to say this again, but I enjoyed making all those sketches. My hand feels like it's about to fall off right now, but I'm happy."

They shared a laugh and she gazed into his eyes, noticing a light there she hadn't witnessed before. "I bet you're ready to go home and rest."

He sat up straight and stretched his arms and back. "You'd think so, but I'm not ready to go back just yet. I think a little more fun is in order to complete the day. What do you say? Want to see the rest of the festival with me?"

Carly's eyes widened. It was the Sweethearts Festival after all and she didn't want people to get the wrong idea. "Oh, I don't know. I need to help Kendall pack everything up."

"I'm almost done here," Kendall called out the RV door. "Go have some fun!"

She felt the blood rush to her cheeks as she turned back to Luc. Now she had no excuses. "All right, I'll stay for a little longer."

Carly walked with Luc to the carnival and started to relax after realizing the crowds were beginning to thin out. They walked down a row of tents with games. There was a fishbowl toss, BB gun target range, balloon dart throw, and a few others. They picked the BB gun game first.

"Okay, here's how to play the game," the man behind the partition said. "Hit four targets and you get a small prize, five for a medium, and all six for a large."

Carly went first. It took her two shots before getting a feel for how to aim the gun. Then she hit three targets and missed the last one. She stomped her foot but chuckled at the same time. "Almost had it. Think I'll try again."

She reached in her pocket, but Luc beat her to the punch, slapping a five-dollar bill on the partition. "How about two more rounds? Keep the extra dollar."

The game operator thanked him and smiled, placing the money in a pouch on his belt before Carly tried again. This time she hit three targets in a row. "Only one more." She grinned while aiming again, but somehow missed the last three. "What? This game has to be rigged." Carly handed Luc the gun, laughing. "Here, you can give it a try."

Luc winked at her while taking the gun. *"Merci, Mademoiselle."* Hearing him speak in French and the ornery quirk of his eyebrow caused more giggles to bubble out of her mouth. She liked this side of him. Luc aimed, missed the first, hit three in a row and miss the last two.

"Nice try," she said, still giggling. "Let's try something else."

They moved on to the fish bowl toss. The point of the game was to toss ping pong balls into the fish bowls to win a betta fish. They were given three tries. "You go first this time." He agreed and missed twice before landing the third ball right in the center bowl. "You did it!" she cheered and leapt into his embrace.

He spun her in a circle before putting her down, giving her a shy smile. "Go ahead and pick out your fish."

"*My* fish?"

Luc chuckled. "Yes, I won him for you. Besides, I already have two cats to look after."

She walked over to the partition and looked over the different colors of fish in the small plastic containers the game operator set out. In the end, she chose a royal blue betta and brought him back over to show Luc. "Thank you for my fish. I think I'll call him Fred."

His lips curved into an amused grin. "Fred?"

"Yes, do you have any better suggestions? Maybe a French name?"

"Francois might suit him."

She studied the fish with all his fancy fins. "I like it. Francois he will be."

Music filtered in from a tent close by and Luc motioned toward it. "Would you like to dance?"

Heat rose to Carly's cheeks as she tried to stall answering his question. "Now look who's being spontaneous."

"Weren't you the one saying I needed some R&R? Well, this is my way of relaxing. Why not take your own advice and join me?" He held his hand out, prompting for her to come with him.

Carly hesitated, trying to ignore the music in the background and the twinkling lights reflecting in his cerulean eyes. If she didn't bow out now, the Elnora Monet would paint her into the scene he was creating—one including them dancing under a sea of stars and twinkling lights. Yet, a small part of her was curious to see how the portrait would turn out. She placed her hand in his, allowing her walls to melt away. "I'll dance with you, but only for one song."

He led her toward the area where couples were dancing, and Carly carefully placed her container with the fish on a table nearby. When she moved into his arms as a slow song started, she forgot any objection to Luc she'd had before. Today he had proven he was much more than his wealth or famous family name. The way he'd jumped in to offer free portraits to help animals find a home showed his generosity and thoughtful nature. Besides that, his talent for art astounded and inspired her. As they rotated in a slow circle, one song turned into two, yet they didn't stop. Carly sketched the moment in her mind—the way his arms felt around her waist, the light in his blue eyes and the curve of his lips as he smiled down at her. Looking at those lips—so inviting now—she struggled to remember why she'd been so opposed to falling for Luc in the first place.

As the second song ended, Luc leaned in closer. Carly's heart pounded, ready to give into her impulse. She closed her eyes, lips expecting to meet his, but instead they made contact with his cheek as he pulled her into an embrace. "I've had a wonderful time with you today, Carly."

"I did, too," she managed before burying her face against his chest to hide her flaming cheeks. Had she somehow misread all the signals he'd been giving?

"I'd like to see you again next weekend. Will you take a tour of the Southern Shores Vineyard with me?"

Carly craned her neck to look up at him and a relieved smile curved on her lips, hardly caring about the location or date. She was only happy Luc seemed unaffected by her impulsive attempt at a kiss. "Sounds perfect."

# 11

Luc's eyes flew open before dawn with the desire to create pounding in his heart. He threw on an old sweatshirt, pants, and shoes, but neglected to comb his hair before heading to his studio. There was no time to waste. Once inside the room, he threw the sheet off his old easel with a wide grin before turning to the portrait of Angeline. "Today's the day, *mon amour.*"

Within a few minutes, Luc had packed up all his paint and art supplies in a carrying case and swung the strap over his shoulder. Before leaving the room, he tucked a canvas under his arm. Luc attempted to shut the door behind him, but gave up and left it open, his other arm occupied carrying the folded easel.

Turning the corner to the main part of the mansion, he met up with Mrs. Potter. She gasped and put her hands over her heart. "Oh, Mr. Belshaw. You scared me half to death! I came early to drop off those forms you requested."

"I'm sorry. I didn't mean to startle you. Since you're here, would you mind opening the door for me?"

Mrs. Potter's forehead crinkled as she studied his face. "Is everything okay?"

He nodded, smiling at her. "Everything is wonderful. Actually, better than ever."

She relaxed and walked with him to open the door. When he made it outside, the dawn had barely arrived. Like Monet, Luc knew how fleeting the sunrise was. He had to paint it as it was happening or he'd miss all the color variations and patterns. It would be a shame to not catch all the tiny details.

When he was a good distance from the mansion, he set up his easel on a ridge overlooking the ocean. He had barely enough time to take out all his supplies as the lights from the sunrise spread across the sky. As his paintbrush stroked across the canvas, creating the array of blues and grays from the ocean and shades of magenta, violet, and tangerine of the sky, Luc felt more alive than he had in years. The technique returned to him as natural as breathing. He was born to paint, and was relieved repressing his talent for two years hadn't allowed it to fade away. Now it burst from him, filling his heart with a joy he hadn't felt in so long.

He added in the ferry in the distance and a few smaller sailboats, taking care to add the shadows they cast over the water. Last, the tan of the sand and forest green of the foliage in his small cove took shape on the canvas.

When Luc finished, he signed the piece, put away his brush, and sat in the grass to observe his artwork. It was one of the finest canvases he'd ever painted of the sunrise, but it hardly compared to the real thing. It was only a duplication of God's artwork. The verse from Psalm 19:1 had always kept him humble in the past, and today it seemed fitting to speak it out loud. "The heavens proclaim the glory of God. The skies display his craftsmanship."

For over two years, he'd spent almost all his time brooding—blaming God for taking Angeline from him. He still didn't understand why it had happened, but for the first time a hint of peace eased the ache in his heart. There was still light and beauty remaining in his life. Luc just had to search a little harder to find it. It was time to move on from his grief.

Luc's mind flashed back to the wonderful afternoon he'd spent with Carly. She'd seemed so closed off and almost annoyed by his presence at first, but that changed as the afternoon went on. He'd wanted to kiss her so badly during the dance, but knew it wouldn't be fair to her—not when his heart still belonged to Angeline. Luc wasn't sure how to explain it to Carly, but hoped inviting her to the vineyard would buy him some time to figure it out. His feelings were growing for her, that much was certain, but just like picking up a paintbrush again had been a step by step process, opening his heart to love again would take time, too.

Luc collected his art supplies, easel, and canvas before heading back inside. Since he was already awake, he had plenty of time to get ready for the church service on Elnora.

Carly was in her white, fluffy robe, singing along with the radio while putting on her makeup when Kendall knocked on the door. "We had another delivery from the flower guy," her sister called.

She chuckled and rolled her eyes. "Another surprise from your Merriweather Hero?"

"No, actually this one is for you."

Carly swung open the door, eyes wide when she took in the large vase full of beautiful flowers. They were a type of orchid she'd never seen before. The petals were a deep shade of purple with blue centers. She took the vase and set it on her end table before opening the attached card.

*Carly,*

*These are Ocean Breeze Orchids. I saw them and thought the blue*

*matches your eyes. They are rare, exquisite, and beautiful like yourself. I'll pick you up on Saturday at ten for brunch at the vineyard.*
*Luc*

Kendall's eyes stared at her expectantly. "Well, give me the details. Who are they from?"

Carly felt heat tingle into her cheeks as she handed her the card. "Who do you think? Who else could have sent this extravagantly expensive arrangement of rare flowers?"

Her sister giggled after reading what Luc wrote. "My little sister's dating a billionaire! I can't believe it."

She swatted Kendall's arm. "Would you stop it? We're not dating. We're just going to tour one of the vineyards on Elnora."

"Well, sorry to tell you, but it sounds an awful lot like a date."

Carly sat on the bed and frowned. "I honestly don't know what to think, sis. I'm surprised he asked me to go at all after what happened when we danced the other night."

Kendall sat on the bed next to her, eyes bright, like a preteen girl talking about boys they had a crush on. "What happened?"

She pursed her lips and sighed, reliving the night's events. "He was sending me all these mixed signals...or maybe I just thought he was. Anyway, I thought he was going to kiss me, but he turned his head at the last second and I ended up kissing his cheek instead."

"Well, that's not too bad. I mean he obviously wants to spend more time with you."

Carly nodded. "I know. It was just embarrassing, you know? To kiss someone who wasn't trying to kiss me."

Her sister gave her a knowing smile. "I'm sorry that happened. Maybe he just needs more time. He is a widower and guys tend to hide their emotions. Maybe he likes you, but isn't ready to move on quite yet. Patience is the key, as they say."

"Yeah, I guess you're right. There's no sense in trying to rush things."

"Yep," Kendall agreed. "Take your time and enjoy learning

about each other. By the way, going to tour a vineyard sounds really romantic."

Carly nodded, but couldn't help letting apprehension get the better of her. "It does, but it makes me nervous that wine will be involved. I mean, he's rich and we're going to tour a vineyard. Wouldn't it be a normal thing to try some of the wine? I haven't had a drink of alcohol since I got into trouble with Alex on Mimosa. I want this to be a new life for me, Kendall."

Her sister frowned and rubbed her chin thoughtfully. "You could ask him to have the date somewhere else."

"I don't want to do that. I'm thrilled he asked me out and don't want to ruin it."

"Well, I guess you'll just have to tell him the truth then if it comes to it. If he really likes you, which I think he does, he'll understand. And if he doesn't, then he wasn't worth your time in the first place."

Carly nodded, smiling at her sister again. "Thanks for the advice. What would I do without you, sis? If I've never said it before, thanks for inviting me to come to the Independence Islands with you."

Kendall pulled her into a tight hug. "You're welcome. Now, we better get ready for work, but tonight, will you let me help you pick out a cute outfit for Saturday? I think your pink spaghetti strap chiffon top would look perfect."

"Yeah, I'd like that."

Kendall stole a glance at Carly's dresser and took a double take. "Is that a betta fish swimming in my favorite lemonade pitcher?"

Carly cringed and nodded. "Yep. I'm sorry. I'll buy a bowl for him soon. I promise."

"Okay, as long as *soon* means tomorrow at the latest."

She couldn't help but laugh as her sister left the room. "Look what you did, Francois! You're already drawing attention to yourself and getting me into trouble."

12

When Saturday arrived, Carly still had a bad case of the jitters. The date she never knew she wanted with Luc was half an hour away, but her hair was still wet, and an unsightly zit had formed in the center of her forehead the day before. Last night, she had applied some of a honey solution recipe she'd found online and put a band aid over it, said a prayer it would work, and went to bed. Now, looking in the mirror, she was relieved to see the swelling had gone down.

Still smiling at her reflection, she reached for the toothpaste in the drawer and put some on her brush. Carly had almost had it in her mouth before noticing the toothpaste smelled spicier than usual. She looked down at the tube and realized it was the heat rub she used for sore back muscles at night. Carly rolled her eyes and proceeded to thoroughly wash out her toothbrush.

*Girl, you've gotta keep your head out of the clouds! Calm down and focus.*

After a successful attempt at brushing her teeth, she applied a little more concealer than usual to cover up the remainder of the blemish and put the rest of her makeup on as usual. Now she just had to dry her hair, curl it, and get dressed.

After a few more minor mishaps, one including burning her finger on the hair curler, Carly dressed in the light pink top her sister picked out and matched it with some light capri pants. Her outfit felt light and airy, perfect for a brunch at the vineyard. She topped it off with a wide brimmed sunhat in case it happened to be a picnic. Carly didn't really know what to expect, but that was the intrigue of the date Luc had planned for them. She loved being spontaneous.

When she made it downstairs, Kendall was at the kitchen table working on some invoices. By some miracle they had no house calls that weekend. Her sister smiled when she saw her. "You look stunning, Carly. I couldn't have picked a better outfit for you if I chose it myself."

Carly crossed her arms and scoffed. "You *did* choose it, silly."

"Oh, yeah. You're right. Well, way to go, me!"

They shared a laugh and Carly put on the sunhat. "Do you think this is too much?"

"No, I think it's perfect. You might want to bring along a cardigan just in case though. I heard a little tropical depression might blow through at some point today."

"Really?" Carly stopped in her tracks. "Rain on my first date with Luc?"

"Oh relax. The weather channel said it probably wouldn't arrive until two. You should be done by then...at least with the brunch part." Kendall stood and gripped Carly's shoulders. "The best sisterly advice I can give is just go with the flow. Even if it rains, your date can still be a memorable experience you'll treasure. Remember my first one with Tyler?"

Carly giggled. "Yeah, the zombie mascara eye disaster. How could I forget?"

Kendall grinned and shook her head. "I was half blind in one eye and couldn't even read the menu. I spent half the evening trying to hide my swollen eye from him, but in spite of that, we had a wonderful time."

"When you say it like that, a little rain doesn't sound all that bad."

"Nope, not at all." A knock sounded at the door and Carly winked at Kendall. "Wish me luck!" They shared a hug before Carly walked to the door and opened it.

Luc stood before her in a light blue button-down shirt and jeans. Carly breathed a sigh of relief, observing his casual look and realizing she'd made appropriate choices for her outfit. Then she noticed the flowers in his hand. "These are for you, Carly. I must say, you look stunning this morning."

She murmured a quick thank you and took the vase full of flowers. They were white roses with blue baby's breath this time. "You're spoiling me," Carly managed when she found her tongue again. "If you keep this up, the whole house is going to be full of flowers."

His eyes twinkled in the morning sun. "What's so wrong with that?"

"I'm going to put these on the counter really quick," she said while turning to hide her grin. He had more charm than she knew how to handle. Carly put the vase on the counter and then tiptoed out.

"Have fun!" her sister whispered as she snuck past.

When Carly returned to the door where Luc waited, her heart rate had finally slowed down. Kendall was right. Whatever happened, she'd go with the flow. Luc had already seen some of her quirky personality when they first met at the mansion and hadn't been scared off by her ill-timed kiss on the cheek. He'd showered her with flower arrangements. Now, Carly just needed to have fun and be herself.

Luc led her to his convertible and held the door open for her. After she sat down, he closed the door after her and went around to the driver's side. After he got in, she gazed at him in surprise. "I assumed you always had a chauffeur drive you places."

He shook his head. "I have been lately because I've been so busy, but there's no need to most of the time when I'm just taking a leisurely drive around the Islands. People recognize me and sometimes stare, but I don't need bodyguards since there's only tourists on Mimosa. It's why I chose to live here. Honestly, the estate is too big and ritzy for me. Most of the rooms are hardly used, but I inherited it and it allows me privacy."

Carly nodded. "That makes sense."

As Luc pulled out of the driveway and onto the road, Carly watched the scenery of Merriweather go by. It was a nice day for a drive with the convertible top down at about seventy degrees. She enjoyed feeling the wind whip through her hair, although she'd spent a long time curling it. At least Luc had seen it before it was all windblown. "So, how's Francois?" he asked. "I hope he's adjusting to his new home well."

"He's good. I don't have a fish bowl yet, but he's enjoying swimming around in a lemonade pitcher for right now. Kendall wasn't very happy with me."

He laughed so hard it made his eyes water. "I can understand why!"

They made small talk while driving through Hopper. It felt so natural, she almost forgot all about Luc's wealth. She would have mistaken him for a normal guy when he wasn't wearing a suit, at his mansion, or riding in a fancy limo.

After crossing the bridge to Elnora, they turned onto the road along the coastline leading southwest. She noticed the turn off for Belshaw Drive as they passed it. "Have you ever toured the South Shores Vineyard before?"

Luc nodded while keeping his eyes on the road. "Yes, I'm friends with Dante's family from way back. He just took over the vineyards. He's been asking me to paint a view of some of the scenery for a while. I've neglected to do so until now."

Her eyes widened. "Until now…as in today?"

He sighed with a grin. "Yes, I shouldn't have said anything. It was supposed to be a surprise, but I've started painting again."

She clasped her hands together. "Luc, that's great news! What prompted all this?"

He ran his fingers through his hair with a chuckle, but kept his attention on the road. "I guess you might say drawing sketches at the festival the other day was God's way of helping me wake up. You were a part of that too, Carly. If I hadn't met you, I don't think I would have been at the festival at all. I probably would have still been sitting in my stagnant mansion feeling sorry for myself."

"Well, I'm glad you came. The truth is, I feel like a part of me has come awake, too. My artistic side. I had forgotten how much I enjoy art until seeing all the pieces in your mansion and hearing about the Monet Museum. I know now that art is meant to be a much bigger part of my life than I realized."

His eyes sparked with excitement and he grinned at her for a moment before returning his attention to the road. "I'm glad to hear you say that, because making art is the theme of this date."

Carly drew in a sharp breath. "What does that mean?"

He grinned while turning onto another road with a sign for the South Shores Vineyard. "You'll see. I don't want to ruin the surprise."

Her heart rate quickened as he drove past the long rows of grapevines. "Luc, you better tell me. You're not going to make me draw or paint in front of a bunch of strangers, are you?"

He shook his head while parking in front of the visitor's center. "No, of course not. This is a private tour. Just relax and have a good time."

Carly shifted uncomfortably in her seat while reaching to unfasten her seatbelt. *Go with the flow. Have fun. Go with the flow. Have fun.* She kept repeating Kendall's words in her head as Luc opened the passenger-side door and led her toward the building. Was Luc telling the truth, or were there a bunch of people waiting inside?

A moment later, Carly breathed a sigh of relief when he led her past the building and turned onto a path leading to a ridge overlooking the vineyards. In a clearing, there were two easels set up with canvases, paints, and a picnic lunch. "See?" he said with a wave of his arm. "There's nothing to be worried about. It's just you, me, and some blank canvases to create on."

Carly giggled as he pulled her into his embrace. "This is amazing. Thank you."

His lips brushed the top of her head before he murmured, "*Tout le plaisir est pour moi, mademoiselle.*"

Carly was glad he held her in his arms, because her knees felt weak all of a sudden. She guessed his words meant something like, "you're welcome," but they sounded more eloquent and romantic in French. What was this guy doing to her?

He held onto her a little tighter and looked down. "Carly, are you feeling all right? You seem unsteady on your feet."

She nodded, regaining her footing before looking up to gaze into his eyes. "Yeah, I think I'm just hungry. I should have had a small breakfast shake before I left the house. I get hypoglycemic when my blood sugar gets a little low sometimes but I'll be fine once I have something to eat." She let out a nervous chuckle, wobbling on her feet a little as he kept one arm around her waist. He guided her to a blanket spread out on the ground with the picnic basket to one side and they sat together. "How did you do all this?" she asked, relieved to be sitting safely on the ground.

"I arranged for my cook to make the food and asked Mrs. Potter to set all this up for us before we arrived. I'm sorry if my surprise was too much for you. For a minute there, I thought you were going to faint on me."

She shook her head, managing a smile. "I'm fine. Really. This is wonderful, Luc."

"I hoped you would think so." He turned to unzip the top of the insulated picnic basket, before starting to set everything out, waving away a few flies as he went. "I wasn't sure what you liked, so I had my cook make a variety."

Carly watched as he set everything out on the blanket. There were bagels, croissants, fried eggs, sausage patties, slices of cheese, and different mini bottles of juices. She waved some more flies away while waiting.

"Sorry about the insects today. If only we had a little wind to scare them away. I guess we'll have to eat quick before they gobble it all up before we can enjoy it."

She chuckled. "I don't think that should be a problem. I'm pretty hungry." Carly watched as he took out four more containers with mixed berries, cream cheese, chocolate drizzle, and another had something resembling ultra-thin tortillas. "What are those?"

He opened the last container to show her. "Traditional French crepes…my grandmother's recipe. You can have them plain or put toppings on them. They taste really good with sweetened cream cheese and fruit."

Carly's eyes rolled back, breathing in the heavenly sweet aroma. "Those look and smell amazing."

He passed out plates, utensils, and napkins before they both chose from the delicious food selections. Carly tried out a crepe topped with cream cheese and mixed berries first, savoring the way the flavors melted together in her mouth. After that, she sampled a little bit of everything. Looking up halfway through the meal, she realized Luc was watching her with an amused grin. She wiped her mouth and furrowed her brow. "What is it? Did I do something weird?"

He shook his head, swatting at a few more annoying flies. "No, I'm just glad you're not afraid to really enjoy your food in front of me. Most of my dates in the past few years just took dainty nibbles of their meals and left most of the food on their plate, afraid of not looking proper or something."

She raised an eyebrow, surprised at the sudden twinge of jealousy that rippled through her. "How many women have you dated recently?"

"Oh, I said that wrong. When I attend charity events or banquets in the public eye, it's usually customary to have a 'date.' These are not romantic dates as you must think. It's just someone to sit with and have a conversation with during the event. Sometimes they are acquaintances or someone my staff finds for me."

She shivered as wings buzzed near her ear and waved the pest away. "I understand now, but have to ask, do you ever get tired of being in the public eye all the time?"

"Yes, more often than I'd like to admit. Especially when I'm away from the Islands or in Paris. I grow weary of people trying to become closer to me just because of my family name. There are good sides to being in the public eye though. I have this ready-made platform to make a difference in the world. So, whenever I find myself getting tired of people and all the things the media says about me and my family, I try to remember that on the flip side, I can still help other people."

"That's a good way to think about it." Carly's heart started to pound, seeing the joy and passion in his eyes when he talked about making a difference. It was the same look he had when hearing about the animals who needed to be adopted.

"So, what about you, Carly? Have you ever thought something you are passionate about could help make a difference in the world, like your artwork?"

She chuckled uncomfortably. "My art? You mean my chicken scratch on poster boards?"

He scoffed and reached over to wave a few more flies away from her plate. "It is certainly not chicken scratch. You have much more God-given talent and potential than you realize, Carly Mulligan."

She turned her head to gaze out over the vineyards. "You know, I always thought I'd go to school at a fine arts college, but when my brother died, I changed my plans. I thought honoring my brother was my new responsibility. I have always loved animals, but I think I was finding a way to mask the pain. A way to put my life on a new path. I don't regret it. I think I'll always enjoy helping my sister with the mobile vet, but the truth is, I want to do so much more than just that."

"So why not do it then?"

She laughed out loud. "That's easier said than done, isn't it?"

"Maybe you're right, but I figured out last Saturday, I'd rather spend my life trying and risk failing, than doing nothing to change the situation."

Carly turned back and smiled at him, appreciating his insight. "That's a good way to think about it."

When they finished their meal, Luc put the rest of the remaining food back in the picnic basket and grinned at her. "Look at that. All the flies are magically gone now that the food's put away."

Carly chuckled. "Yeah, I can't imagine why."

"So, are you ready for your first lesson in painting with the Elnora Monet?"

She nodded. "I thought you'd never ask."

# 13

Carly watched the rows of grapevines take shape on her canvas, under Luc's patient tutelage. She'd painted before in college, but the objects were always from stills set up in the classroom. This was dramatically different.

"See how the lights and shadows have already changed since we started?" Luc asked while mixing another color on his palette.

"Yes."

"Even if you draw the same scene at a different hour or different day, you'll never create the same painting. Also, two different artists will have their own impression of what they're painting. While I might see a certain shade of green, your eyes might see it as a slightly different shade. It's all about perspective."

Carly studied their two almost completed paintings in amazement. She had learned more from Luc in under an hour than she'd learned during any art class in college. "I never thought of that before."

After a few more strokes, they both finished their masterpieces. "Now, to sign," he said, and with a flourish of his brush, he shaped the letters, signing simply, 'Luc.'

Carly signed her name too before standing back to look at both canvases. "You're right. Both our paintings are completely unique." She turned to him with a contented sigh. "Thank you for today, Luc. I've had such a good time."

"The date's not over yet. We still haven't actually toured the vineyards, have we?"

She shook her head. "No, I guess we haven't." He offered his arm and started to lead her down an adjacent path leading down the ridge. They'd taken a few steps before remembering their artwork. "Shouldn't we put the paintings somewhere? I don't want them getting ruined."

"Don't worry about that. I've arranged for everything to be taken back home."

She chuckled to herself as they continued walking. "I guess I should have known you'd have everything worked out." Only Luc Belshaw could make a well-planned date at a vineyard seem completely spontaneous. She thought any other girl sharing a perfect day with someone like him would have just been absorbed in the magical moments, but Carly's mind reeled, wondering how he made every aspect of their brunch date flow seamlessly.

"This vineyard has been owned by the Greco family for generations. They came here from Italy," he explained as they walked down the rows of grapevines. "My father has known Angelo and Maria Greco from when we spent summers here on Elnora when I was a child. Now their son Dante is taking over and wants to expand it. I would introduce you to him, but he's out of town this weekend." He pointed to a hill in the distance. "See the newer construction? That's a project he's been working on."

Carly nodded, noticing a few cabins and a large meeting hall taking shape. "I hope it turns profitable for them. This whole place is amazing. I've always wanted to visit Italy, and I feel like I'm actually there right now."

He smiled. "Is that where you'd like to go when you save enough money? That was our deal, right? That you'd actually go abroad sometime in the near future?"

"Maybe," Carly said, grinning. "I haven't decided yet."

The whole tour took about an hour and they finished up inside the building with the winepress and then walked back out to a garden surrounded by mature trees. In the center was a small table set up with a basket full of different cheeses and bread. There were also two bottles chilling in a pail of ice and two wine glasses. At the sight of them, Carly's stomach tied into knots. Now was the time to reveal the truth and hope it didn't ruin the date. "Um...Luc, this is all wonderful, but I have to tell you something," she started as he pulled a chair out for her.

He took a seat across from her, his blue eyes attentive. "What is it? I hope this date hasn't been too over the top. I tend to do that."

She shook her head, letting out a nervous laugh. "No, it's nothing like that. I've had a wonderful day with you, but do you remember what I told you about my rebellious stage after my brother's death?"

Luc furrowed his brow, leaning closer. "Yes, I remember."

"Well, since recommitting my heart to Jesus, I haven't had a drink of alcohol. It became a real problem in my life, and I'm afraid if I have even a little it might tempt me to revert to my old bad habits."

His shoulders relaxed as he reached for the bottle. "I completely understand. The truth is, I don't drink either. My father is a recovering alcoholic and it's an addiction I never want to fall into. That is why the Greco family makes this non-alcoholic wine specially for me. I had two kinds of it brought in for us to enjoy today."

Carly felt the knots in her stomach unwind. "I had no idea that even existed."

"Yes, they use a special filtration process to remove the alcohol after it is made."

Her eyes widened in amazement. "I guess you learn something new every day. It turns out I was nervous to tell you for nothing."

He reached for her hand and kissed it before looking up at her with a serious expression. "Carly, I never want you to feel like you have to hide things from me. Whatever it is, just tell me the truth, and I'll do my best to be understanding. I hope you'll do the same for me as well."

She nodded, feeling like her heart would pound out of her chest. "I will."

"Good." He released her hand and motioned toward the spread on the table. "Well, I hope you've worked up an appetite from walking around the vineyard. This bread and cheese was made by my cook as well and it's some of the best I've ever tasted."

"I'm famished," she admitted as he opened the bottle of sparkling grape juice and poured them both a glass. She took hers and lifted it. "So, what should we toast to?"

Luc tilted his head in thought for a moment before lifting his glass as well. "To new adventures."

"New adventures," Carly repeated and they clinked their glasses together before taking a drink. Just being with Luc was an adventure in itself and she couldn't wait for the next chapter.

They made small talk while finishing their refreshments. Then Luc invited her to come up the hill with him to look at Dante's new projects. It was a long walk and they stopped after crossing the vineyard and sat on a rock wall. "We can rest here for a few minutes." Luc said. "The trek up the hill is a long one. Besides, there's something I need to tell you, too. I was going to tell you after our date, but since you were so open with me, I thought now would be a good time."

Carly studied his serious expression, half of her glad he wanted to start out their relationship with honesty, and the other half, terrified of what he would tell her. Things had been going well—almost too well. In her experience with dating, when things seemed to be going too smoothly, it was because there was some kind of catch. "What is it?" she asked, cringing inside.

"I'm the oldest son in the Belshaw family and with that comes responsibilities."

"What kind of responsibilities?"

"Well, the most pressing one is, I'm expected to inherit my father's company after he passes. Lately his health has been declining more rapidly than expected…liver issues from his heavy drinking years. So, I might be taking over sooner than I thought."

She gave him a knowing smile. "That must be hard for you. I'm sorry to hear about your father."

He nodded. "It is tough. I want to spend time with him before he gets any worse, but I'm afraid he'll be disappointed in me."

"Why would he be disappointed? Doesn't he notice how successful you've made the hotels here in the US? The one on Hilton Head is amazing. When you take over, I imagine all the hotels around the world will continue doing great, if not better under your leadership."

His eyes gazed into hers and she could see the sadness in them shining through. "I don't want to take over the company. I'm fine with the responsibilities I have now, but if I took over, I'd be ten times as busy as I am now. My father has always known this. I've been passionate about art for most of my life, but he's never approved."

"You told me you have a younger brother. Could he help with some of the responsibility?"

"Yes, Pierre has always been more like my father. He loves the business side of things. He lives and breathes it, in fact."

"Well, that could work then. If you have to take over, share the load with him."

Luc nodded, but his eyes were still sad. "I have no doubt he would, but that's not the biggest issue. Taking over the company involves me moving to Paris."

Carly stayed silent for a few moments as his words sank in. Even after she replayed them in her head, they didn't make sense at first. The realization finally came, slowly and then all at once. She'd found the perfect guy, but soon he might be an ocean away from her. "I see," she said. "But what about your life here?"

Luc shrugged. "Like I said, I haven't decided yet. I'll be traveling to Paris in a few weeks to visit my father. I'm hoping we'll be able to work something out. After all, I still do have to manage the hotels I have here in the States. Plus, the staff at my estate on Elnora would have to be reduced since I wouldn't be living here full time. Some of them would lose their jobs."

Carly's eyes drifted away from him, to a few dark clouds forming on the horizon. "That's unfortunate."

"Yes, it is, but the worst part will be spending so much time away from you." He touched her cheek before moving her face to look at him again. "My feelings for you are growing, Carly. I know this is happening fast, but I feel like myself again when we're together. You make me laugh and you make me dream for things I thought I'd never dream about again."

She felt a tear dripping down her cheek. "I feel the same way, but how would this work if we're thousands of miles away from each other?"

"I don't know, but would you be willing to try and work this problem out together?"

She choked on her tears as thunder rumbled in the distance. "I need to think." She stood from the rock wall and began walking down the rows of grapevines again, but now the beauty of them seemed muted.

"Carly, wait," Luc called from behind.

She blocked out his voice as he continued to call for her. She picked up her pace until her speed walk turned into a run. The wind picked up, causing the vines to sway back and forth, morphing into clawed hands trying to grab her. Why had she allowed Luc to draw her in when deep down she had feared from the beginning he would hurt her? Now she felt vulnerable and weak for letting him have a place in her heart.

The rain started blowing in with the wind, pelting her skin like porcupine needles and turning the dirt beneath her into mud, but she continued running. She'd reached the middle when the pelting rain turned into a downpour. Her feet slipped and she fell into the mud, losing her shoe. She reached blindly for it, the rain and her own tears obscuring her view.

"Carly, are you all right?" Luc's voice asked from behind her.

"I'm fine," she sniffled, wiping her wet face in vain. More water only dripped down her forehead and into her eyes. She couldn't seem to escape him. "I just want to go home."

"Let me help you." He reached down, retrieved her sandal and then helped her stand after she'd put it back on her foot. She tried to move past him, but he gripped her shoulders. "Would you please hear me out?"

She blinked through her tears as the rain pelted down on them. "I always do this, Luc. I always fall for guys who aren't good for me, or ones I can't have. It's better that we end this now, before we both get hurt."

He shook his head. "No. It's too late for that."

"Too late?"

He took in a few deep breaths, winded from chasing her. "It's too late because I'm already falling for you, Carly. I want to see where this journey leads. So, you see, I can't let you go. I can't. No matter what happens, I want to make this work somehow, but that can only happen if you're willing to give us a chance."

Carly stared at him for a few long moments as the rain chilled them to the bone. Was she willing to risk her heart for something truly wonderful with Luc? She nodded, knowing she did. He was worth the risk.

Luc took her nod as a cue and pulled her into his embrace, caressing her cheek before their lips met. Carly forgot all about the cold rain drenching them. She felt warm and safe in Luc's strong arms and never wanted him to let go.

# 1 4

Luc brought Carly home in the late afternoon. It was still pouring outside, their clothes were soaking wet, and Carly's pants were stained with mud. However, they were both smiling from ear to ear when Kendall opened the door for them. Kendall gasped at the sight of them. "What happened to you two?"

Luc spoke up first. "I'm sorry for dripping all over your floor. We were caught in the rain and Carly slipped in a mud puddle."

Kendall chuckled, looking them over again. "I can see that. Wait here and I'll get some towels."

"I'll be heading right out, so please don't get one for me. Just Carly, please."

After Kendall walked out of sight, he pulled Carly into his arms and gave her a tender kiss. "I'll see you soon."

"Not soon enough," Carly whispered, pulling him in for another kiss. "Would you like to join us at the church on Merriweather tomorrow morning?"

He nodded. "I'd love to. See you then." He kissed her hand before heading out the door and rushing to his car before he became even more soaked by the rain. All the way home, he couldn't stop smiling. The date with Carly had been amazing. Even though he almost scared her away with talk of moving to Paris, it had ended well, with a passionate kiss in the rain he wouldn't soon forget.

When he entered the mansion, he was met by his secretary, holding a clipboard and pen. She opened her mouth, as though she wanted to ask him a business question, before noticing his odd appearance. "Mr. Belshaw, you're soaked to the bone!"

He chuckled, realizing she'd observed a lot of odd behavior out of him during the past few weeks. She probably worried he was losing his mind. "I'm fine," he assured. "I'm just going to go upstairs and change into some dry clothes. Is there anything urgent?"

"Your father called."

"Thank you." He glanced at his watch, calculating the time difference. It was well past midnight in Paris. "He'll be asleep by now. I'll call him tomorrow morning."

Luc went upstairs and felt much more comfortable after drying off and putting on new clothes. He had just settled into the lounge chair in his room when Athena came through the cat door he'd had installed recently to avoid keeping his bedroom door propped open all the time. She curled around his legs before leaping into his lap. "Well, good afternoon. Happy to see me? Sorry I've been gone all day." He heard the cat door swing again and was surprised to see Descartes enter, too. He glanced around the room timidly before hiding behind some furniture. Luc sighed with a smile. His hostility had melted away for the most part, but he knew it would take time and patience for the cat to trust him.

Athena curled up on his lap and fell asleep purring, causing him to grow drowsy, too. He'd barely started to drift off when the intercom beeped and Mrs. Potter's voice came through.

"Your father has called again. He said it can't wait and is waiting on line one."

Luc sighed and mashed the intercom button. "Thank you. I'll talk to him now." He gently transferred Athena to the floor and shuffled across the room to retrieve the phone. "Good evening, Father. Why are you up so late?"

"I've been trying to reach you all day. Where have you been?" His voice bristled with authority.

Luc sat on the edge of the bed and raked his fingers through his hair. His father liked to have him on a short leash. "I was out. You know I shut my cell phone off when I have important appointments so I won't be disturbed." It wasn't exactly a lie. He considered his date with Carly as a very important appointment.

He heard his father cough and clear his throat. When he spoke again, he was calmer. "I wanted to know if you've considered coming for the banquet at Pyramide du Louvre soon. Everyone will be there and I had hoped to announce you as my successor."

Luc shook his head, although he knew his father couldn't see him. "We've had this conversation before. I hadn't planned on coming this year, and I haven't decided if I want to take over the company yet. I need more time to think. I'll speak with you about it more in the summer when I fly to Paris."

There was a long pause as his father coughed before speaking again. "You've had too much time already." His voice was low and raspy, sending guilt rippling through him. Luc knew his indecisive behavior was causing his father stress, but he couldn't help it. Taking over an entire company was a huge decision—one he didn't take lightly—especially now with the new developments in his relationship with Carly. "Will you at least consider coming for the banquet? I would like to see you, even if there will be no announcement."

"When is it scheduled?"

"The middle of next month. I'll have my secretary send over the specific details. Your brother has some announcements of his own he'd like you to be present for as well."

Luc agreed to satisfy his father and then said his goodbyes. All the previous joy he'd had after his date with Carly faded away. He'd always loved visiting Paris, but living there was a whole different experience. He needed some advice and knew exactly who to ask.

Soon he was in his office with his mother on video conference. She sat in the living room with her huge bookcase in the background and sipping on a mug of steaming coffee. It made him feel like he was sitting in the house with her, having a casual conversation like usual.

"So, how was your date with this Carly girl? I knew from the first time you mentioned her there was something that intrigued you about her."

He shook his head as she boasted. "You do know me pretty well."

"I'm supposed to. That's what mothers do. They teach, observe, and give advice, that is, if their children are still willing to listen."

"The date went perfectly. Well, almost. We got caught out in the rain at the end, but I really didn't mind."

"Oh, I see. A kiss in the rain sounds romantic."

His heart started to race. "How did you know? Mother, you didn't find out Carly's number and call or something, did you?"

"No, of course not. Just relax. I learned the error of my ways when I meddled before. It was just a lucky guess. You seem to really like her, and a vineyard is a nice place to have a first kiss, so I thought it might happen today."

"You'll always be a hopeless romantic, won't you?"

She nodded while taking another sip of her coffee. "Sure will. It saddens me things didn't work out between your father and me though. Sometimes I wonder what things would have been like if I'd tried harder. Maybe he would have gotten the help he needed sooner…"

"He left you," Luc interrupted, his earlier frustration returning. "Actually, he left all of us. He chose his career and his addiction over us time and time again. Now he wants me to choose the same kind of life he chose to lead."

She nodded. "Is that why you wanted to talk? Is your father pressuring you about the company again?"

Luc nodded, lowering his voice. After all, it wasn't his mother he was frustrated with. "I don't want to live in Paris. My whole life is here…my career, you, and now Carly. I would be miserable there."

A huge smile spread across her face. She placed her coffee cup off to the side and clapped her hands. "Good for you, Luc! You've finally decided what you want."

He nodded. "I think deep down I've always known my place was here, but it doesn't change the fact that I have responsibilities to the family. It wouldn't be right to abandon them."

"You would never abandon them. That's not the kind of person you are. You can still be involved in the company, but not have to shoulder all the responsibility. When you go to Paris, speak to your brother and find a solution together. We don't live in the dark ages and we're not royalty, although sometimes I think your father seems to think so."

They shared a chuckle. "Yes, Father wouldn't object to sitting on a throne and ordering people around, would he?"

She nodded with a sigh. "What I'm trying to say is, just because you are the first born doesn't mean you *have* to inherit the company, but you can still play a big part in its growth and legacy."

Luc leaned back in his chair, his shoulders beginning to relax. "You're right. I never thought of it that way, Mother. Thank you."

"You're very welcome." She smiled and blew him a kiss,

causing him to laugh. "Now, when am I going to meet this new love interest of yours? I hope *before* you leave for Paris?"

Carly was thrilled when Luc asked her to go to Hilton Head to meet his mother after church on Sunday. He explained the next few weeks would be busy, including two out of town business trips, so it would probably be a while until she had a chance to spend much time with him. She rode with him after church, but was surprised when they headed in the direction of Elnora. "Where are we going? Wouldn't it be quicker to just take the ferry here on Merriweather?"

He just grinned and continued driving. "I know of a shortcut."

Carly sat in silence, thinking over his answer for a while before understanding what he was saying. "We're taking the helicopter?"

"Yes, it's much quicker."

"Really? I've always wanted to fly in a helicopter!" She leaned over and kissed his cheek.

He let out a nervous chuckle and kept his attention on the road. "I just hope you still think so when we're over the ocean."

About thirty minutes later, when they lifted off from the platform on the roof of his mansion, she started to realize what he meant. It was crazy and exhilarating being so high up in the air. She closed her eyes and clung to Luc when the helicopter tilted to turn a different direction. Butterflies fluttered in her stomach and she felt dizzy at first, but before too long she gathered enough courage to look out the window. "It's amazing! I thought it would be much louder in here. I always see people with headphones on to block the noise in the movies."

He motioned toward the interior. "There's sound proofing in the walls of the cabin to reduce the sound. It doesn't take it away completely, but makes for a much more enjoyable ride. I asked the pilot to take us over the Islands so you could see what they look like from the air."

She looked out the window again in anticipation. She saw the last bit of Elnora pass by and the bridge before they were over the bunny shaped island called Hooper. She pointed out the window, heart racing in excitement as they flew over Merriweather. "Wow, look at that! You can see the drive where I live...and there's Reginald Square, and Pirate's Cove! Do you see them?"

"I'll take your word for it."

Carly looked over at him, noticing him gulp and grip the armrest. "Are you afraid of heights?" He nodded with a fake smile and she stared at him in astonishment. "Then why do you fly in a helicopter?"

He shrugged and his shoulders started to relax. "It's the fastest transportation to the mainland. If I don't think about it too much, I'm fine."

"Don't worry. I'll hold your hand," she said with a chuckle while weaving her fingers through his and kissing his cheek.

His eyebrow quirked in amusement. "Thanks, I feel much better now."

"How long will it take us to get to Hilton Head?"

"About half an hour or so."

"Really? That quick?"

He chuckled at all her questions and his blue eyes twinkled. "Yes, I told you it was a shortcut." She cuddled against him and watched out his window as miles of ocean passed by. She loved experiencing new things with Luc by her side. It was like each day was a new and unexpected adventure.

When they neared Hilton Head Island, Carly sat up and looked out her window. She'd gotten used to the tilting motion of the helicopter and it no longer made her feel dizzy. It was a convenient way to travel, and Carly knew it would be a huge let down the next time she had to take the long ferry ride to the mainland.

They traveled up the coastline until they reached a gated beach front property. When they landed on the helipad, a two-story house with a wraparound screened in porch came into view. It was a stunning property, and a bigger house than she'd ever lived in. However, after seeing Luc's mansion, seeing the modest house he'd grown up in was surprising. It was no wonder he was wealthy but remained humble and generous. His mother had raised him in as normal a setting as she could.

Luc helped her step down from the helicopter and they held hands while walking up the stone path to the house. His mother came out to greet them before they reached the front steps and hugged Carly right away. "Welcome! I'm so glad you could come on such short notice."

Luc hugged his mom before introducing them. "Carly, this is my mother, Nina Kirkland."

"It's so nice to meet you."

Nina smiled. "You too. Luc has told me so much about you." She held the door open and motioned for them to come inside. "Come and make yourself at home. I have some finger foods in the living room."

Carly walked into the house, enjoying the traditional layout of everything. It had a warm feeling, making her feel welcome and comfortable right away. When she sat on the sofa next to Luc, she noticed one of his paintings right away. Nina had also displayed pictures of Luc and his brother on her wall. They ranged from adorable baby pictures, to older ones of them graduating high school. Judging from the uniforms they wore in their school pictures, Carly could tell they'd gone to a private school. It was really no surprise, since their family name was so well-known.

After Nina sat across from them, they prayed over the food. Afterwards, they enjoyed little finger sandwiches, fruit, and lemonade while making small talk. Luc's mom had a pleasant personality, putting her at ease. "So, Luc tells me you are passionate about art like him," Nina said while pouring herself another glass of lemonade.

Carly nodded. "Yes, I have been since I can remember. In class when I was supposed to be taking notes, I'd often be doodling."

"Yes, I remember seeing Luc's notebooks full of little doodles, too. I suppose a true artist can never stop practicing their craft, even when they're supposed to be concentrating on something else."

"Yes, I agree. I went to school to be a vet assistant, but I minored in art. The art classes I took were the highlight of my college years."

"You sound so much like Luc. He's always had a hunger to learn about art. When we're done eating, I'll show you some photo albums from when he was growing up. There are a lot of him creating something. He was always busy."

"I'd love to see them."

"No, Mother. Please, don't bring out the albums," Luc begged.

Carly chuckled, seeing Luc cover his face and his ears grow red from embarrassment. She nudged his shoulder playfully. "Oh, don't be so dramatic! Besides, whenever you meet my parents my mom will show you all my embarrassing pictures, too."

Luc nodded in agreement, but let out a reluctant sigh. "All right. Go ahead, if you must."

"Yay!" Carly cheered, before kissing his cheek. "I can't wait."

# 15

"Your mother is so wonderful," Carly commented when they returned to the Belshaw Estate after touring the rest of Hilton Head and eating out for dinner.

Luc held her hand as they made their way down the stairs from the roof of the west wing. "She thinks a lot of you, too. In fact, her exact words before we left were 'she's a keeper.'"

"I'm glad she thinks so."

"Well, good, because I do, too."

Carly smiled and turned to face him when they reached the bottom of the stairs. "This whole weekend has felt like a dream. How am I going to go three days without seeing you?"

He smiled and pulled her close, resting his forehead against hers. "My business trip in Chicago will go by quickly, I hope. Until then, I want you to think about something for me."

"What's that?"

"Why don't we go to my studio and talk there in private? I've made some changes I wanted to show you anyway."

She nodded, heart pounding as they crossed through the main part of the house and over into the east wing. There, Athena and Descartes came out of their room. Athena ran over right away and started to purr while rubbing against Carly's legs. She leaned down to pet the cat, her anxiety momentarily melting away. "I've missed you, sweet girl, but you seem so happy."

Luc chuckled while watching them. "She follows me all over the mansion. I've never seen such an affectionate cat."

"So, she's managed to turn you into a cat person after all?"

"Yes, I think she may have."

She looked over at Descartes eyeing her cautiously from a few feet away. "And how's he doing?"

"Descartes follows Athena wherever she goes. He's still cautious, but is coming around slowly. I had a cat door installed in my room so they can come and go as they please."

"That's great. I'm glad to see they are both doing so well."

After petting Athena a little longer, they walked to his studio together. When Carly entered, she couldn't stop staring at the walls in wonder. It looked so different since she'd last stepped inside, with all the sheets removed from the paintings. The shades were open now and the entire room was filled with light and color. There were paintings from famous places all over the world—all places Luc had traveled and recreated the experience with his paintbrush.

"It's stunning, Luc. When did you uncover them all?"

"A few weeks ago. When you uncovered Angeline's portrait, it forced me to face the pain I harbored inside." He motioned toward the other paintings displayed on the wall. "After the initial sting faded away, I was able to uncover the other paintings, and last, the easel."

Carly hid her face from him as the embarrassing memory returned. "I still don't know what caused me to go snooping where I didn't belong. It's very unlike me."

He stepped closer and lifted her chin so she had to look at him. "It was meant to be. I didn't realize it at the time, but God sent you here for a reason. I was going through the motions...

still traveling and taking care of business like usual...but on the inside I wasn't really living at all. I realize that now. He sent you here to wake me up."

She smiled up at him, happy tears forming in her eyes. "I'm happy to be your alarm clock any time."

He laughed and outlined the curved of her cheek with his thumb. "You are an incredible woman, Carly Mulligan. You've brought laughter and joy back into my life when I thought it was gone forever. It's become clear to me, God meant for us to be together."

Carly stood speechless as he leaned in to kiss her. She melted in his arms, enjoying the tingle of his lips moving over hers and the warmth of his arms wrapped around her. She'd gone from despising him to caring deeply for him in such a short period of time, but were things moving a little too fast? Her previous fears and doubts came crashing around her again, like waves pounding the sand. Carly still didn't know if he planned to move to Paris or not. She didn't like having doubts—not when everything seemed to be going so well. However, the fact remained, the closer she got to Luc, the more she risked heartbreak if things didn't work out. After the kiss, she leaned back to look at him, heart pounding. "You said you wanted to tell me something earlier?"

Luc nodded. "Yes, I have to visit my father in Paris sooner than I thought."

She stepped back to study his expression. "What does that mean? Is it good or bad?"

"It's good, actually." She observed some of the previous torment in his eyes from speaking about the situation had faded. "I'm finally going to tell him I still want to help in certain aspects of the company...namely here in the US, but I don't want to inherit the company or move to Paris. I'm going to tell him once and for all, my place is here."

Carly stared at him, dumbfounded. She'd been anticipating

bad news, but this was good. Or had she heard him wrong? "You're not moving to Paris?"

A smile played on Luc's lips as he nodded. "No, I'm not moving to Paris. I'm staying here with you."

She rushed into his arms again, laughing and crying tears of joy. "Oh, Luc. Those are the most beautiful words I've ever heard."

He kissed Carly's head and held her close. "There's just one more thing I need to ask you."

She stepped back to look at him, wiping her tears. "What?"

"When I go visit my father next month, there's going to be a company banquet at the Pyramide du Louvre with shareholders and franchise owners from all over the world. It's one of those occasions I was mentioning where it's customary to have a date."

Carly chuckled. "Are you asking me for permission to hire a beautiful woman to hang off your arm at the banquet?"

He shook his head. "No, I want you to come with me. You'd have a chance to meet my family in Paris and travel abroad like you've dreamed. We can take my private jet and stay in one of the finest hotel suites in Europe, all expenses paid. We'd have separate rooms of course. Oh, and a custom gown would be designed for the occasion. Mrs. Potter would have to send over your measurements to the designer in Paris in advance. We'd even squeeze in some time to enjoy the sights. You still have your passport from when you went to Cancun, right?" Luc paused when she didn't answer and shook his head. "I'm sorry. I'm getting ahead of myself. You haven't even said yes yet, and I'm already planning the itinerary."

It was Carly's turn to be shocked again as she attempted to process his words. Paris, private jet, banquet, custom gown, finest hotel in Europe—all the words swirled in her head like a category five hurricane. "Luc, I don't know," she finally managed to force out of her mouth. "This is a lot to think about."

He nodded and took her hands in his. "I know, and I'm sorry to throw it all at you at the same time, but I would like you to be there with me. I believe with you by my side, I'll have more confidence to tell my father how I really feel about taking over the business."

"I would love to be there to support you and meet your family, Luc. I just need some time to find out if it's even possible for me to go. I can't abandon Kendall on a whim. I'd need to find someone to help her with the clinic while I'm away. That will not be an easy feat."

"Of course. I'd be willing to help pay for a temporary assistant. I also have connections, remember?" He paused to wink at her. "It shouldn't be a problem to find someone in time."

Carly grinned at him with an exasperated sigh. "Jean-Luc Belshaw, you are making it very hard for me to say no to this spontaneous trip halfway around the world."

He lifted one of her hands and kissed it. "Then say yes!"

"Paris!" Kendall's high-pitched squeal almost popped Carly's eardrum. "He asked you to go to Paris with him all expenses paid and you said you'd have to think about it?"

Carly sat on the couch and held her head in her hands to stop the bedroom from spinning. "I can't just leave you here alone. What kind of sister does that?"

"You said yourself, he offered to hire a temporary assistant for us."

"Yeah, but this is crazy!" Carly stood up and began to pace. "Don't you see how crazy this is? I practically just met this guy and now I'm taking a trip to Paris with him?"

Giggles bubbled out of Kendall's mouth. "This, from the girl who brags about being spontaneous. Are you freaking out because the billionaire you met is more spontaneous than you?"

Carly picked up a couch pillow and tossed it at her sister's face, causing Kendall to giggle even harder. "You're not helping at all."

Kendall stifled her laughter, expression turning serious again. "All joking aside, this is a once in a lifetime opportunity. I mean, how often do you get asked to go on an all-expenses-paid trip to Paris? You'll also be taking the trip with someone you care deeply for, right?"

Carly nodded. "You're right. I do. I've never felt this way about anyone before."

Her sister leaned against the couch cushions with a contented grin. "Then I think you already know your answer."

She paused to bite her nails for a minute as the idea became more settled in her mind. "That only leaves one very important question. Maybe you can help me with that one though."

"Sure, just say the word."

A wide grin curved on Carly's lips. "What on earth am I going to wear for the trip?"

Kendall's eyes grew wide as saucers. "So, you're going?"

Carly nodded, feet dancing their way back to the couch. She hugged her sister and let out a squeal of excitement. "Yes, I'm going to Paris!"

# 16

Luc's business trip slogged by as he attended meeting after meeting to discuss the opening of a new hotel in Chicago. While he always took meetings seriously, the three days full of them all melded together. On the second day, he received a text from Carly while taking a break for lunch.

HAVE YOU FOUND ANY TIME FOR R&R, LIKE YOU PROMISED? OR ARE YOU BEING A WORKAHOLIC? IF YOU ARE, I JUST MIGHT NOT BE ABLE TO HOLD UP MY END OF THE DEAL AND GO WITH YOU TO PARIS. JUST SAYING...

He grinned, picturing her probing eyes, making sure he lived up to his word. I'M GOING TO FIT SOME IN TODAY. THOUGHT OF GOING TO SEE THE CLOUD GATE AND THE SKY DECK AT THE WILLIS TOWER.

GOOD FOR YOU! I THOUGHT YOU WERE AFRAID OF HEIGHTS?

Luc chuckled before texting back. DON'T REMIND ME.

OH, YOU'LL BE FINE. HAVE FUN AND TAKE SOME PICTURES FOR ME.

I WILL. Luc smiled and shook his head. Carly's playful banter had put him in a brighter mood. He glanced at the time on his phone before sliding it into his pocket. He had an hour and a half before his next meeting. After lunch, he'd planned on going back to his hotel room to go over his notes one more time before his next meeting, but it wasn't really necessary. He knew the agenda of the meeting like the back of his hand. Instead, he'd squeeze in time for R&R like Carly suggested.

His scheduler, Ms. Peters, tried to snag him on the way out the door. "Mr. Belshaw, do you have a moment to speak with the financial department from New York? They've been calling since before lunch."

Luc shook his head. "I have another appointment I can't miss. Please schedule it for this evening after my last meeting."

"An appointment?" The young woman's brown eyes stared at him through her thick glasses in confusion before scrolling through the agenda on her tablet, no doubt wondering if she'd missed something.

He gave her a guilty smile. "I'm sorry for the confusion, Ms. Peters. It's something that just came up. I'll be back before the next meeting." Luc walked away, leaving her still scrolling on her tablet, rearranging things with a flustered look on her face. For a moment, he felt bad for causing the poor scheduler extra stress, but he quickly swept the thought away. Carly was right. He did need to make time for himself occasionally.

While Luc was away on his business trip, Carly spent most of her free time making a list for things she might need on the trip to Paris and using an app on her phone to learn some basic French words and phrases. She even brushed up on French art and history for good measure. The thought of meeting Luc's father and brother tangled her nerves up like a roll of yarn. He had mentioned his father was a difficult man to get along with sometimes. Still, she thought being well-prepared would help boost her confidence and make a good impression.

On Tuesday, Luc sent her pictures of his sightseeing excursion like he promised. There was even one of him standing on the sky deck of the Willis tower. She chuckled at first, because he looked like a little kid on a field trip, but it also made her heart ache a little. He would only be gone one more day, but she missed him like crazy. When they brought the clinic home for the evening, Carly took the car to go visit Descartes and Athena to give them some attention like she'd promised.

When she reached the front gate, the guard welcomed her with a smile. "*Bonjour*, Ms. Mulligan. No need to show me your ID."

She smiled back at him, glad he had warmed up to her since their first meeting. She'd become a common sight at the mansion lately. "*Merci*, Monsieur Corbin."

He nodded while mashing the button to open the gates.

Once inside, even the butler was friendly toward Carly and allowed her to walk right back to Descartes and Athena's room without having to wait for Mrs. Potter. She opened the door to the room, pleased to see the two cats grooming each other on top of the kitty condo. Athena spotted her right away and bounded over as best as she could with her back leg in the cast. She rubbed against Carly's legs and purred loud as a motor boat. "Glad to see you're doing well, pretty girl. I think we can remove your cast next week. Are you happy to hear that?" Athena responded by purring even louder. Carly was pleased to see her coat still looked well-groomed without any signs of new mats forming.

After petting Athena, she looked over at Descartes. "And how are you doing? You look as handsome and feisty as ever." Descartes rubbed up against the cat condo, keeping his distance, but at least he didn't growl and hiss like the first time she met him. Carly took a bag of cat treats out of her purse and shook them. "Come here, boy. I know you like these."

Descartes ignored her until she started giving Athena some

treats. She continued paying attention to the Himalayan while watching him out of the corner of her eye. Descartes slinked over, inch by inch until he was almost adjacent with his friend.

Carly avoided looking at him while gently tossing a morsel in his direction. He moved forward just enough to gobble down the treat. She smiled and threw a few more, closer each time he'd eat one. Before too long, he was within reach. Carly kept one in her palm and held it out. "Come on, boy. You can do it."

He sniffed the treat and backed up at first, emitting a brief growl, but the smell of the treat persuaded him in the end. Descartes not only ate the treat, but he rubbed his head against her hand twice before walking away. Carly's heart felt like it would burst. He was finally warming up to her. It was a good sign that with time he would warm up to Luc as well.

She finished petting Athena before standing to leave, when Mrs. Potter peeked her head through the open door. "I was hoping I'd catch you before you left, Carly. I need to send over your measurements to Paris for your banquet gown. Luc also had a few sample dresses brought over so you can choose what kind of style fits you best.

Carly gulped, hearing about the unexpected task before her. It would be like attending her senior prom, but with a bunch of paparazzi and socialites scrutinizing her every move. All of a sudden, the reality sank in. She was really going with Luc to Paris and would meet his family in the process. What if they didn't like her? What if they convinced Luc she wasn't good enough for him?

Mrs. Potter's voice cut through the cloud of doubts swirling in her mind. "Are you all right, Carly? We can schedule this for another time this week if we need to."

"No, it's fine. I can spare a few minutes." Carly followed the secretary into the main part of the mansion, past where Luc's office was. They walked into a guest room with a four-poster king sized bed. She looked around in amazement, observing the vaulted ceiling, chandelier, and balcony with an ocean view. It had to be ten times as big as her room at the beach house. If the guest room was this grand, she couldn't help wondering how elaborate Luc's room was. She walked into the closet to look at the gowns hanging in there. As her hands brushed over the silk, organza, and satin fabrics, Carly didn't like the doubt slowly creeping up in her mind. She'd never thought of herself as having simple tastes until seeing Luc's mansion. It was all so extravagant, while she was used to a simpler way of life. Would she fit into Luc's world?

"I know this must be overwhelming for you," Mrs. Potter said.

Carly turned to meet the secretary's knowing brown eyes. "Just a little." She paused and released a sigh while taking a seat on a nearby ottoman, unexpected tears pricking her eyes. "Okay, maybe it's overwhelming me a lot."

Mrs. Potter pulled up a little stool across from her and offered a gentle smile. "It's completely normal for you to be feeling this way. Believe it or not, it's a big relief to all of us here at Mr. Belshaw's estate that you do seem a little reluctant to take this all on in the future."

Carly wiped her eyes with the back of her sleeve and sniffled. "Relieved? I don't understand. I had started to believe everyone was beginning to like me. Even the guard has been kinder to me recently."

Mrs. Potter patted her hand. "That's not what I meant at all. We're happy that Mr. Belshaw found someone like you. Someone who could make him laugh and enjoy life again. We were worried someone would come along and charm him, but only pretend to love him because of his wealth. Whether you see it or not, your 'normal' ways are good for Luc. I've never seen him so happy...after Angeline's passing, that is."

She managed a shaky smile. "Really? Sometimes I wonder if our differences of upbringing will come between us someday."

She motioned to the extravagant room they were in. "I mean how do I ever get used to all this? The closet in this room alone has to be the size of my bedroom on Merriweather."

The secretary chuckled. "It will be a huge adjustment, but you'll grow used to it. Don't focus on the huge estate. Just think about a room at a time. Each one has a purpose for a larger cause. For example, this one is to make any guests who come here to feel comfortable as possible. We've hosted delegates from all over the world in this guest room when we have charity events. Mr. Belshaw always thinks of the comfort of others, and his charities give back to the community."

"I didn't think about it that way. You're right. Luc is very generous with his wealth. His charities are a cause I can definitely get behind."

"I had hoped you would come to that conclusion. Which reminds me, I've been wanting to thank you, Carly. Actually, all of us here at the estate have wanted to thank you. Mr. Belshaw is a special person to us and we're glad he is finding happiness again. After Angeline's death, a cloud of gloom spread over this place. Who knew he needed a feisty New Englander to come snooping around to lift it?"

"Well, I'm happy to snoop more often if it will help."

Mrs. Potter laughed with her. "Yes, snoop away whenever you'd like." After they'd both calmed down enough to speak clearly again, the secretary sighed. "In all seriousness, we do hope things between you and Luc work out. A word of caution when you travel to Paris, though. Please try not to take to heart about how Mr. Belshaw's father might act toward you. He is a brilliant man when it comes to running a business, but sometimes blunt and overly critical."

Carly nodded. "Luc mentioned he was a little difficult to get along with."

"Yes, and he probably will not approve of his son dating an American, either."

She crossed her arms and sighed. "Is this supposed to make me feel better?"

Mrs. Potter shook her head. "What I'm trying to say is, it's important for you to stand your ground. He will accept your new relationship with his son eventually, once he realizes how happy you are together."

"I sure hope so." Carly released a deep sigh and touched a dress with silky blue fabric. "I think I'm ready to try on some dresses now."

# 17

The moment Carly arrived back home, Kendall met her in the hallway, cheeks flushed. "There you are! I was starting to get worried when you didn't answer your phone."

"You called? I didn't even hear my cell ring." She reached into her purse and pulled out the phone, studying the blank screen. "Well, that explains it. My phone's completely dead. I'm sorry, sis."

"Oh, it's all right. It's just…well, Mom is freaking out. Have you happened to see what was on the news?"

"No, I hate watching it, besides finding out about the weather. What is it?"

Kendall starting tapping out something on her phone and then handed it to her. "Here, I found the same story online."

Carly took the phone from her sister and the headline on the news story made her mouth hinge open. *Jean-Luc Belshaw Jr. and His New American Girlfriend Spotted Dining at Hilton Head Island.* "I can't believe this! I didn't see any paparazzi or camera flashes when we went out last week."

Kendall reached for her phone again and scrolled down, eyes scanning the story again. "It says here, the original source was from a customer at the same restaurant who snapped the photo. That's why there was a delay before it circulated through the news."

When the reality finally had a chance to marinate, she drew in a sharp breath. "Mom saw it, didn't she?"

Kendall nodded with furrowed eyebrows. "Yes, I'm afraid so. Now, Mom *and* Dad have decided to come down for a short weekend visit. They said they missed us and it has nothing to do with the billionaire you're dating, but I don't believe them."

Carly's breath came in short ragged gasps. "I'm supposed to be preparing for the Paris trip, and we're both busy keeping up with all the business at the clinic. This couldn't be happening at a worse time." She moved into the kitchen and took a seat at the table, resting her head in her hands.

Kendall sat in the adjacent chair and placed a comforting hand on her shoulder. "It'll be fine. They were bound to find out eventually. Also, Mom sounded pretty excited about you dating a billionaire."

Carly groaned. "Yeah, that's the problem. She's going to be all googly-eyed around Luc since he's famous, and Dad is going to give him 'the talk.'" She buried her face deeper in her palms, dreading it with every fiber of her being. All of a sudden it was like they were back in high school, about to go to prom before her dad pulled her date into the other room to show him his shotgun collection. He'd scared quite a few of her dates away by doing that.

Kendall giggled. "Tyler got that treatment, too. Well, sort of. Since dad wasn't here, he got 'the talk' from Mom. He'll probably get a second talk from Dad when he comes back from overseas."

She turned her head to peek at Kendall. "Yeah, I guess you're right. This is just not the way I wanted them to find out, you know? And now, I'm going to have to explain this whole trip to Paris."

"Yeah, I didn't plan on the way Mom met Tyler either. She was skeptical at first, but it all worked out. It will work out for you, too. You'll see. They might give him a hard time at first, but Luc's good qualities will shine through."

Carly nodded, sitting back in her chair with a sigh. "You're right. I'm probably worrying for nothing." She took her phone out of her pocket and managed a nervous grin. "Guess I better call Mom and then Luc to warn him. No telling how fast this news story will go international. His dad doesn't exactly know about me yet, either. The next few days and weeks could get very interesting. Wish me luck."

Kendall stood and pulled her into a hug. "I'll do better than that, sis. I'll pray."

Luc arrived back on Elnora on Wednesday evening, too exhausted to do anything but crawl into bed, but Carly's phone call from the day before still resonated in his mind. She'd warned him about the news story soon enough for him to call his father before he caught wind of their new relationship. He'd wanted to tell him about her and introduce her to him at the same time, but that wasn't to be. Now, he knew and would have time to already form an opinion about Carly before they met in person. It was a less than ideal situation, but he would have to work with it regardless.

Then came the surprise of meeting Carly's parents next week. Her voice sounded stressed while apologizing for their unexpected visit, even though Luc assured her he was excited about the prospect of meeting them. It would show him another side of Carly's life he'd never witnessed before. Luc wondered what made her so reluctant about their meeting, but drowsily pushed the thought away for the moment. He would need a day to recover from his trip before thinking about how to approach that situation. Meeting Carly's parents was an important step and he wanted to make a good impression.

Luc rested on his stomach, bunched up the pillow under his head, and closed his eyes, relishing the comfort of his own bed. He had almost fallen asleep when he felt the light pressure of paws on the mattress beside him and whiskers tickling his nose. He peeked through one eyelid and let out a groggy chuckle, seeing two glowing cat eyes staring back at him. "*Pardon, douce petite mademoiselle.* I neglected to greet you when I came home, didn't I?"

Athena purred and rubbed against his fist that was holding onto the pillow.

He opened his hand, rubbing her behind the ears. "Miss me?"

She purred like a motorboat and started to drool.

After petting Athena for a few minutes, he felt something jump onto the end of the bed. He squinted in the dim light and saw the outline of Descartes crouching by his feet. "*Bonjour, monsieur.* Did you miss me, too?"

Descartes recoiled at the sound of his voice, but didn't jump off. His glowing eyes watched him cautiously.

"It's all right. You can keep your distance if you'd like. I won't rush you. Goodnight, Descartes."

The cat lowered his body in a slow graceful motion, tucking his feet underneath him and closing his eyes. Luc couldn't be sure. It was hard to hear much of anything over 'Athena the motorboat,' as he'd started to call her, but he thought he heard the tiniest purr out of the temperamental Angora cat. Then after a moment Descartes rested his head on Luc's foot under the sheet and he felt the warmth and vibration from his throat.

Luc rested his head back on the pillow and a smile curved on his lips. He never dreamed he'd allow a cat in his room at night —nonetheless two—but he found their presence comforting, Athena and Descartes were like little vibrating space heaters, lulling him into a blissful sleep.

Carly held Athena carefully as Kendall cut the cast off the cat's back leg. When the cast was completely removed, she placed Athena back on the exam table while her sister observed the way she stood and moved on it. Athena wasted no time turning to lick fur that had been hidden under the cast for several weeks. She rubbed up against Kendall's hand and purred, as if saying thank you.

A smile curved on her sister's lips as she rubbed Athena behind the ears. "I bet that feels a lot better, doesn't it, girl?"

Luc laughed from beside Carly as Athena purred even louder. "Now do you see why I've been calling her Athena the Motorboat?"

She leaned her head against his shoulder, chuckling with him. "Yes, I do. She's louder than ever."

Kendall picked the cat up, cuddling her close before handing her over to Luc. "She should be good as new now. Her leg seems to have healed perfectly. Descartes might not be able to keep up with her as well anymore."

Luc held Athena close to him as she massaged his arm, looking content to be held by her owner. "Thank you for taking such good care of her. She really has grown on me, I must admit."

Kendall nodded. "I can see that. It appears she's quite fond of you, too." She turned back to Carly. "I'm going to take the clinic home for the evening."

"All right. I'll have Luc's driver bring me home in a little while."

After her sister agreed, Carly walked out of the clinic with Luc, who still held Athena in his arms. Once inside the mansion, they took her back to the cat room where Descartes was waiting for them. The moment Luc put Athena down, the cats greeted each other with purrs and nose sniffs. Athena laid down in front of him with her belly in the air and paws batting at him, ready to play.

They shared a laugh while watching them wrestle and romp around the room for a few minutes. A few minutes later, Carly followed Luc down the hallway to his studio. Cuddling on the oversized divan by the bay window, they watched the colors from the sunset begin to fill the sky. It had been about a week since his return, but they'd both been so busy, Carly had hardly seen him.

His lips brushed against her temple. "When will your parents be here?"

Carly sighed, resting her head against the inside of his shoulder as his arms held her a little tighter. "Two days from now. I'm supposed to pick them up on Saturday afternoon."

"Are they staying with you and Kendall?"

She shook her head. "They're planning on staying at a hotel on Mimosa. Our house just isn't big enough."

He leaned his cheek against her head with a sigh. "Is it too late to cancel their reservation?"

"I don't know. Why do you ask?" She sat halfway up to meet his eyes.

"I was thinking it might be nice for them to stay in one of my guest rooms."

Carly sat the rest of the way up and scoffed. "Are you crazy? It will be like an interrogation twenty-four-seven. You won't be able to get away from them."

He shrugged. "I've got nothing to hide. They can ask me anything they want."

She shook her head and stood, beginning to pace. "I don't think you understand."

Luc sat on the edge of the chair, watching her with a raised brow. "Why are you so opposed to me meeting your parents?"

Carly stopped and looked at him then, seeing the hurt in his eyes. "I'm sorry. It's not like what you think. I do want you to meet them. It's just, they've never liked anyone I've brought home before. What if they bring up our age difference, or the fact we come from different backgrounds? What if they bring up your wealth and my lack thereof, or say we aren't right for each other?"

Luc leaned forward and ran his fingers through his dark hair before meeting her gaze again. "Are these fears really about your parents? Or are they your own doubts about this relationship?"

Carly stood rooted to the ground, mouth agape. His question had shot through her like an arrow, piercing the core of her insecurities. She took a moment to compose herself before responding. "Luc, I can't pretend those issues haven't crossed my mind the past few weeks. Our upbringings are dramatically different. You and I both have to acknowledge that. I've had to work really hard for everything I have. My parents were able to save up some money for my college tuition, but for the rest I had to get student loans. Loans I'm still paying on. Kendall and I have a house payment and a tight budget each week…"

"And I've had everything handed to me on a silver platter," Luc interrupted, his eyes downcast. "Is that the point you're trying to make?"

Carly sighed and crossed the room to sit next to him again. "No, I didn't mean to make it sound like that. I know you've worked hard to improve your family's company. You're not at all who I thought you were when I first came here. I judged without offering you a chance."

His sad, weary expression was replaced with a boyish grin. "You thought I was a reclusive self-absorbed, old miser."

Carl rolled her eyes playfully. "Well, I *was* right about one thing. You were a little reclusive."

"Perhaps." Luc chuckled while weaving his fingers through hers. "I just needed someone special to remind me there were still things to look forward to in life. I'm thankful that person was you."

"I'm thankful you came into my life, too." She gazed into his blue eyes, remembering why she'd fallen for him so quickly. Everything seemed right with the world when he was with her. He made her smile, laugh, create, and dream for things she never knew she wanted. If only she didn't have so many doubts in his absence.

Luc lifted her hand and kissed it, causing butterflies to flutter in her stomach. "Carly, I know our pasts and lifestyles are different as night and day, but we have a lot in common. We both have faith in God, which I consider the most important. I think religion was one thing that tore my parents' marriage apart. My mother always had a strong faith, but it was never a priority for my father. For a while, after Angeline's death, I started to act more like him in that aspect. I blamed God and stopped attending church, but now I'm glad He forgave me and helped me turn back to Him."

"Me too." Carly wiped a stray tear from her eye, amazed by his conviction and honesty. It took a brave man to admit he had been struggling to turn back onto the right path.

Luc nodded before continuing. "We have more in common than just faith. We have our love of art, nature, animals, and humor...among other things. My family's position and responsibilities may cause some complications, but that doesn't mean we should give up."

Carly squeezed his hand, wondering why she'd ever felt so conflicted before. "I think you're right, Luc," she admitted. "But I need to tell you one more insecurity I've been struggling with."

"What's that?"

Carly bit her lip, hesitating, but she wanted to be honest. "I've never been in a serious relationship. I know it sounds shallow of me, but I've never committed to anyone before. It's always just been a few dates. Any nice guys who wanted to see me again...well, I always pushed them away, convincing myself they'd break my heart in the end." She dropped her eyes from his gaze and traced the flower design on the divan. "I guess you could say I self-sabotage relationships."

Silence hung in the air until Luc lifted her chin. When their eyes met, Luc gave her a gentle smile. "In case you haven't noticed, *ma chérie*, our relationship is far deeper than just a few dates. Like an annoying fly at our first picnic, you can't just swat me away. I'll keep coming back."

Carly smiled through her tears. "I don't want to swat you away."

"Good." He pulled her in for a long passionate kiss, chasing all her worries away. When he leaned back to look at her again, she struggled to catch her breath. "So, now that we resolved that, are you still opposed to inviting your parents to stay here?"

"No, not in the least. You can invite them for the entire month if you want," she said with a breathless chuckle before clutching the edges of his shirt collar to pull him in for another kiss.

# 18

On Saturday afternoon, Luc and Carly sat in the helicopter across from Mr. and Mrs. Mulligan en route to Elnora. While Carly was reluctant about his chosen mode of transportation at first, Luc convinced her it would be the most convenient way to travel back to Elnora after their long plane ride. Watching them stare out the window in wonder confirmed he'd made the right decision. "My cook will have lunch prepared for us when we arrive," he said as they started traveling over the water. "There will be salad, bread sticks, and choices of clam chowder or vegetable beef stew."

Mrs. Mulligan's face lit up at the mention of the soups. "Clam chowder is my favorite and vegetable beef is my husband's. Carly, did you tell him that?"

She grinned from beside him with a nod. "I wanted you both to be as comfortable as possible. The clam chowder Luc's cook makes is amazing. I've never tasted the vegetable soup, but I'm sure it's delicious, too."

Mr. Mulligan turned to him with a nod. "I appreciate all you've done to make us feel at home."

"You're welcome, sir."

"Carly tells me you've got quite a collection of classic cars in your garage."

Luc nodded. "I'd be happy to show them to you after lunch."

"I'd like that."

When they landed on the helipad, a valet took their suitcases inside, and Luc led the way through the west wing into the main part of the mansion. From there, they journeyed into the grand formal dining room.

He watched Carly's interior designer mother in amusement as she admired the French architecture and chandelier hanging down over the long table. "The space is breathtaking. I've never seen anything like it."

"Thank you. My grandfather had the middle section of the estate built in the 1920's and passed it down to my father, and he added on the east and west wings. I never dreamed it would one day belong to me, but here we are. I've been meaning to add some updates to the older section of the house on the upper level but keep the charm of the place intact. Maybe you could offer some of your expertise."

Mrs. Mulligan smiled as she took a seat at the table next to her husband. "I'd be happy to."

Carly squeezed Luc's hand after taking her place next to him, reassuring him things were going well so far.

After church on Sunday, Luc invited everyone, including Kendall, Tiff, and her children over for a picnic lunch at his private beach. It turned out to be a beautiful day in the high seventies. Although the water was still too cold for swimming, the kids enjoyed wading in ankle-deep surf and collecting shells while Zoe chased them around with happy barks. Kendall and Tiff sat together on a large picnic blanket watching them, laughing at the dog, and enjoying some girl talk.

Carly sat in a beach chair beside her mother while Luc and her dad were out in the garage again talking about cars while lunch was being prepared. "How was your first night at the mansion?"

Her mother let out a contented sigh while leaning back in her chair. "Oh, it was wonderful. The bed was so comfortable, I fell asleep the moment my head hit the pillow. It was so much better than staying at a hotel with outdated décor and noisy guests next door."

"I bet. I'm glad you're enjoying yourself so far."

"We are, and your father and I are pretty impressed with Luc. I think you've found yourself a keeper, Carly."

She grinned seeing Luc and her dad returning to the beach, one carrying a picnic basket and the other with a cooler of drinks. If not for the mansion in the background and the unseasonably warm day in early April, it would have seemed like the normal picnics on the beach she used to have in Massachusetts when she was a child.

Luc and her father set the food and drinks on a nearby blanket before calling everyone to come pray over the food. Afterwards, everyone picked out their sandwiches, bags of chips, and soda. Carly and her mom picked tuna sandwiches, opened their chips, and started putting them in between the bread.

Luc chuckled while sitting in the chair beside Carly. "Are you both putting chips in your sandwiches?"

She nodded, arching her eyebrow at him while taking a bite and washing it down with some orange pop before speaking. "Yeah, don't you? It keeps them from blowing away and adds an extra salty crunch."

He shook his head with another laugh. "Never heard of it."

"You should try it. Shouldn't he, Mom?"

Mrs. Mulligan peered over at him with a wide smile. "Yes, you should." She turned back to Carly and released a happy sigh. "This reminds me of the picnics we used to have together at Nantasket Beach. You kids used to have so much fun making sand castles and wading out in the water."

Carly nodded. "I was thinking about that, too. Do you remember that one day when the seagull swooped down and took off with my sandwich?"

Her mom laughed. "Yes, I do. I guess he liked the chips in the sandwich, too. At least Kevin was kind enough to share half his sandwich with you."

Carly nodded. "He was always such a good big brother. I miss him."

Her mom dabbed at her eyes and nodded. "Me too. On my last visit here, I happened to see some surfers and thought of Kevin. He would have loved it out here."

"Yeah, he would have."

Her mom composed herself and turned to Luc. "Do you surf?"

He shook his head. "No, ma'am. Not for a long time, anyway. When I was a teenager, I tried it a few times, but I'd always have to be cautious of people recognizing me on public beaches. I've always enjoyed living by the ocean though. It's peaceful."

"I agree. We've lived in the city for so long, I never thought we would want to leave, but now that we're getting close to retirement age, we've been talking more about making a change."

Luc nodded with a smile. "George was just telling me you were thinking of moving here to the Islands."

Carly, who had just taken another bite of her sandwich, almost choked on it. She coughed and sputtered before taking a drink of her pop. She looked at her mother in surprise. "How long have you and Dad been thinking about that?"

Her mom waved away the question with a guilty smile. "Yes, we've been talking about it. I didn't know your father was going to blab about it already." She watched as her father took a seat next to Kendall on the beach and released a faint chuckle. "That man couldn't keep a secret very long, even if his life depended on it."

"So, you're really considering moving here?"

She nodded. "Yes, we think it will be a wonderful place to retire. We no longer have any close family living in Boston. You and Kendall both live here now. In the future we hope to watch our grandchildren grow up and be close to them."

Heat rose to Carly's cheeks. "Mom, neither one of us are even married yet."

"Still, I have a feeling that will soon change." She patted Carly's arm and winked.

Carly stole a glance at Luc who was occupied watching the children play on the beach, acting oblivious to her mother's comment, but she could see a faint smile curve on his lips.

On Monday morning, Carly sat next to Luc in his helicopter, resting her head against his chest. She was both a little sad and relieved after taking her parents back to the airport. It had been a short, but wonderful visit and Luc had made a good first impression with them—most surprisingly with her father.

Luc wrapped his arm around her shoulder and kissed the top of her head. "Deep in thought, *ma chérie?*"

Carly grinned against him, hearing the term of endearment. After brushing up on her French to prepare for their trip to Paris, she'd discovered it meant "my sweetheart." It would have given her goosebumps hearing him say it in English, but in French it made her heart flutter and skip a beat. "I was thinking about you, actually."

She heard a chuckle rumble through his chest. "Me?"

"Yes. I was so nervous about my parents coming, but it turns out there was no need. I believe you charmed them from the moment they got off the plane."

"Oh, I don't know about all that. Your dad still gave me 'the talk,' as you call it."

Carly sat up to look into his eyes, biting her lip. "He did? When?"

He nodded with a boyish grin. "When we were looking at my car collection again on Sunday."

"I thought it seemed a little fishy he wanted to see the cars a second time. What did he say?"

"Well, we talked about a number of things, namely about our trip to Paris. I assured him I would be the perfect gentleman and we would be staying in separate rooms. However, in the end, it all boiled down to him wanting to know my intentions with his daughter."

"How embarrassing!" Carly covered her face, trying to hide her flaming cheeks. When she spoke again, it was through her hands. "I'm sorry, Luc. He used to do that to my high school boyfriends. What did you say?"

"I told him the truth."

She dropped her hands from her face and looked up at him. "And what is that?"

He brushed a few strands of loose blonde hair from her cheek and gulped hard all of a sudden, like his nerves had gotten the better of him for once. "I told him our relationship is still very new, but in that short time I have developed deep feelings for you. The feelings were a surprise for me since I've lost love before and never expected to find it again. I told him I intend…"

"You told him you love me?" she interrupted, her eyes growing wide and heart thumping like the propellers of the helicopter.

He nodded, his fingers outlining the curve of her face as a nervous chuckle escaped his lips. "It just slipped out. I don't think I realized the truth until I said it out loud to your father."

His misty blue eyes gazed into hers, drawing her into a trance. "But what I told him is true, *mon amour*. Deeply, madly, and truly. I love you, Carly Mulligan."

She stared at him for a few long seconds and then her eyes shifted to the blue sky outside the window, still trying to process his words. It was almost like her soul had drifted outside the helicopter and floated out the window. Luc was still in the cabin, gazing lovingly into her eyes and her paralyzed body sat next to him, lips frozen together.

*Say something! Anything!* She screamed at herself from the outside and tried to pound on the window, but the paralyzed Carly didn't hear her.

Had he really just said all the things she never knew she always wanted him to say? The thought sounded ridiculous in her mind, but it was true. She'd never expected to find someone as wonderful as Luc, nonetheless have the courage to not push him away when things became serious. Now, here he was, saying so many wonderful things to her and she literally didn't possess the power to respond.

"Carly? Are you feeling all right?"

All of a sudden, she was back in the helicopter with Luc. She blinked hard, focusing on his worried gaze. He had been waiting for her response for who knew how long while she was off in la la land. "Sorry, I feel a little dizzy and nauseous," she finally managed to croak out while beginning to shiver.

He removed his blazer and draped it around her shoulders before wrapping his arm around her. "Here, just rest against me. It's probably motion sickness."

She did as he suggested, enjoying his warmth and the calming sound of his heartbeat. It should have been one of the best moments of her life. Why couldn't she seem to pull herself together? "Thank you," she said through quivering lips.

"You're welcome. Did you eat breakfast this morning?"

She pursed her lips, trying to remember. "No, I think I was in such a hurry to get to your house on time I forgot."

"That must be what's wrong. We'll land within ten minutes and I'll get you something to eat."

She thanked him and continued resting in his arms. His concern for her was an endearing quality and it warmed her heart. When they reached the mansion, she still felt a little dizzy, so Luc helped her out of the helicopter before sweeping her into his arms.

Carly let out a small gasp of shock. "What are you doing? I'm pretty sure I can still walk."

He grinned while proceeding to carry her down the steps. "Just because you can, doesn't mean you have to. Sometimes it's all right to let someone take care of you."

She grinned and planted a kiss on his cheek. "My knight in shining armor."

He carried her through the west wing, earning some strange looks from a few of the staff, but he didn't seem to mind. They passed through the main part of the house and entered into a small sitting room with a divan by the window. He helped her lay down on the long cushion before pulling a blanket from the top of it and draping it over her. Luc kissed her forehead and smiled. "I'll go find some orange juice and ask the cook to whip you up an omelet or something."

She shook her head. "Oh, orange juice will be fine. I don't have time to eat a proper breakfast. Kendall is expecting me at the clinic by ten."

His eyebrows furrowed. "No, I have to insist. I'll have Mrs. Potter call and explain you're going to be late. I'm not letting you out of my sight until you feel better."

Carly chuckled softly. "Feeling bossy today, are we?"

"I guess so, but for a good cause. I'll be right back." Luc's face relaxed before he left the room. Maybe hearing her still joking around eased his mind she was going to be all right.

Carly smiled while studying the exquisite architecture of the sitting room as she waited for Luc to return with the orange juice. Almost passing out in front of him had been embarrassing, but she had to admit, it was nice having someone take care of her. Carly's smile only lasted for a moment before her mind tangled into knots. She remembered what Luc had said in the helicopter before she felt sick. He loved her. Now, the question was, did she love him?

# 19

Luc had one more business trip to New York a few days before they were scheduled to leave for Paris. This time, he was only gone for two days. In a way, it was good he had to go out of town because it gave him some much-needed time to think. Things had fallen back into a normal routine since Carly's parents went home, but she acted as though he'd never admitted his love for her in the helicopter. He blamed it on her hypoglycemic episode ruining the moment, but Luc was puzzled why she'd never brought it back up after feeling better.

After returning from New York on Friday, he requested his pilot stop by Hilton Head. Soon, he was sitting with his mother on her private dock, sipping glasses of homemade raspberry iced tea. He watched the gentle waves in the inlet, marveling at how the light reflected off it like a million tiny crystals. "Do you think it was a mistake to admit my love for her so soon? Should I have waited?"

She leaned forward in her chair and patted his shoulder. "You were honest, Luc. I don't think honesty is ever a mistake. Has she canceled going to Paris with you?"

"No, she still seems excited about it."

His mother smiled. "Well, that's a good sign. Sometimes women need a little time to know their own hearts. Be patient with her and she will share her true feelings in time."

Luc nodded. "I will. She's worth waiting for."

His mother patted his cheek. "Now there's the gentleman I raised. I'm so proud and happy for you." She leaned back and sighed, her expression turning serious. "After Angeline's death, I worried you would never be the same. I prayed for you every day and now I'm overjoyed to see you come alive again with Carly by your side. I think those scars from the past will always be there, but you're stronger because of them."

"Thank you. I know God answered your prayers."

She dabbed at her eyes before taking a sip of her tea. "So, when are you leaving?"

"Monday, and we'll be there for five days."

She nodded. "That should leave some time for you to show Carly the sights. I'm sure she'll love Paris."

He grinned, remembering his previous excitement about the trip. The fact Carly was going with him, and she would be looking at everything for the first time brought joy to his heart. He would have so much to show her. "Yes, I have some surprises planned. I want to make her first trip to Europe special."

"Have you given any more thought to what you're going to say to your father?"

Luc nodded and turned serious, feeling a knot forming between his shoulder blades. "I have. But I'll have to speak with Pierre in person before making any final decisions. I want Father to know I still care about the company and want to see it grow and prosper. I don't want him to feel like I'm abandoning him."

She offered him a knowing smile. "The best thing is to be honest and stand your ground. He might not take it well when you first tell him, but he'll come around eventually. I think having Carly with you will strengthen your resolve and remind you of one of the many reasons you want to live here in the States instead of France."

He nodded. "You're right. I think it will, too."

When it was time to go, his mother hugged him tight and didn't let go for a while. "I'll be praying for God to strengthen you and give you wisdom…and also that your father's heart will soften to hear what you have to say."

"Thank you, Mother. I feel better already."

The weekend before the Paris trip, Carly felt like she was drowning in preparations. She and Kendall had met the girl who would be acting as vet assistant while she was away. Her name was Alicia. She was on spring break during her last year of vet school and seemed well qualified. Plus, she seemed to get along great with her sister. Luc had done a wonderful job utilizing his connections in Savannah and it was great she lived nearby, too.

Now, it was time to pack. After a little planning, Carly selected sleeveless styles and capris until remembering it would be colder in France than on the Islands. "You're hopeless, Carly," she groaned, putting the clothes away and setting off in search of her boxes of warmer clothes she had stored in the closet. Soon she had piles of long-sleeved blouses, cardigans, dress pants, skinny jeans, a few dresses, scarves, and three pairs of shoes. Afterwards, she stuffed as much as she could into her large rolling suitcase. After rearranging them several times, the bag still wouldn't zip. She took out two outfits and tried again. "Come on!" she grunted while sitting on top of the bag and struggling with the zipper.

"What are you doing?" her sister asked with a chuckle as she came into the room.

"What does it look like?" she said through clenched teeth, still battling the zipper. "This piece of junk refuses to close!"

Kendall walked closer, tilting her head to inspect the problem. "Here, let me take a look."

Carly shook her head, starting to feel dizzy from all the exertion. "No, I've almost got it."

"You're going to break the zipper and then what are you going to do? Carry all your stuff in trash bags?"

Carly threw her hands in the air, releasing an exasperated sigh as she climbed off the bag. It sprang open, sending outfits flying out with it. "Have at it, sis. I'm going to go find my carry on and passport." When Carly returned a few minutes later, Kendall was busy rolling up one last outfit before placing it in the bag. Her mouth hinged open as she zipped it shut with ease. "How in the world? Did you really get everything to fit?"

Kendall nodded with a pleased grin. "You'd be amazed at how many things you can stuff into your shoes. I also rolled up all your outfits together, so you can just pull them out and be ready to go for the day."

Carly's blood sizzled, exasperated that everything seemed to come so easily for Kendall, organization-wise. She almost let out a smart retort, but held her tongue. After all, her sister had only been trying to help. "Thank you," she forced out. "Now, if I can only roll them up as nicely as you did to bring them home."

Kendall gave her an impish grin. "I'm sure sitting on it will work eventually, if you try hard enough."

She gave her sister's shoulder a playful punch and they both laughed. "I really appreciate your help. Sorry I was being a grouch."

Kendall walked over and gave her a hug. "It's all right. I'm sure this whole trip has your nerves on edge, but will you try to remember something for me?"

"What?"

"To relax and try to have some fun. This is a once in a lifetime trip with Luc after all, right? The guy you're crazy about who just happens to be a billionaire?"

Carly chuckled as she released her. "Yes. That's him." She sat on her bed and furrowed her brow, remembering their conversation a couple of days ago. "He told me he loved me...well actually he told Dad he loved me first. Can you believe that?"

Her sister's eyes grew wide as sand dollars. "When did this happen? What did you say? Do you love him, too?"

Carly put out her hands to calm her sister down. "One question at a time, all right?"

"Sorry for getting so excited. Okay, I won't rush you."

She let out a deep breath and met her sister's attentive gaze, deciding to just blurt out the answers all at once. "It happened last Monday after Mom and Dad left. I...I didn't say anything... and yes."

"You love him and you didn't say it back? Why?"

"It's complicated..." Carly's mind flashed back to the awkward moment in the helicopter, shaking her head. "You remember that low blood sugar episode I had...when Mrs. Potter called to say I'd be late to work?"

"Oh, I remember now." Kendall rested her chin in her palm, like she was absorbing all the information she'd just heard. "So, he said he loved you and you didn't say it back because everything went horribly wrong? Now you don't know how to bring it up again?"

She nodded slowly, biting her lip. "Basically, yes. When he said it, I was so shocked, I didn't know what to say. I've never felt this way about anyone in my life, and being in love is scary enough for me, not to mention being in love with a billionaire. There's no rule book for that. How am I supposed to know how to deal with this?"

Kendall took her hand and patted it gently. "There's no rule book for being in love *period*, Carly. But the Bible does tell us what perfect love looks like. It's patient and kind. It's not rude or selfish. It keeps no record of wrong..."

She listened to the rest of the passage from 1 Corinthians 13, realizing she was right. God had set some guidelines for love. "But what if I can't live up to all those?"

Kendall smiled. "This describes God's perfect love. We can try our best, but we'll never quite live up to them. Still, He gives us an example of how love is supposed to look. That's why it's so important to keep God in the relationship. He is the one who helps us continue to strive for those standards. Yes, the fact he's a billionaire does complicate things. But don't forget, underneath all the wealth and fame, Luc is just a normal person like all of us. If you really love him, don't let something like his wealth scare you away."

Carly felt all the puzzle pieces start to fit together in her mind. She did love Luc, and it would be the worst mistake of her life if she didn't take a chance to be with him. "Thank you, Kendall. Now I just have to gather the courage to tell him how I really feel."

"You can do it. Be honest with him. He'll understand."

She nodded and a wide smile spread across her face. "I love Luc! I can't believe I just said that out loud."

Kendall pulled her into another hug and they both squealed at her new revelation. "And I can't believe my sister is in love with a billionaire!"

## 20

On Thursday, Carly could barely contain herself as she boarded Luc's luxury Gulfstream jet. It was the most luxurious plane she'd ever seen. The main cabin featured spacious leather reclining seats with electronic adjusters, pull out trays, and a flat screen television. Behind them to the right, there was a door to a lavatory and beyond a divider, she could see a dining area with matching leather seats and a table, but she didn't want to venture into the other room yet. She would save it for later, whenever Luc wanted to show her around.

While settling into her seat next to Luc, Carly marveled at the luxurious details of the plane, feeling like she was stuck in a dream. She had never particularly enjoyed flying but traveling to Paris in a luxury jet wouldn't be bad at all, especially with Luc by her side. In fact, she'd probably forget they were flying at all.

Luc weaved his fingers through hers, causing goosebumps to travel up her arms. "Nervous?"

"Maybe a little, but I can't wait to go on this new adventure with you."

"Me too."

Carly squeezed his hand a little tighter. She wanted to tell him what was truly in her heart, but needed to find the perfect moment to do it. For now, she decided to simply enjoy being with him.

As the pilot did his pre-flight checks, a flight attendant came by asking if they'd like refreshments before lifting off. She asked for an orange soda and Luc ordered some sparkling cider. When the attendant returned, Carly chuckled, seeing her orange soda in a fancy crystal wine glass. "Everything is luxurious on this plane, isn't it?"

Luc sipped on his drink and nodded. "Why not? It's going to be a long flight. We might as well be comfortable."

A few minutes later, the plane took its position on the runway. Carly looked out one of the large oval windows as the plane picked up speed and lifted effortlessly off the ground. "We're already in the air? It doesn't even feel like we're flying. I thought it would seem a little more jarring, like my flight to Cancun."

Luc nodded and lifted her hand to kiss it. "It's a lot different than a commercial airliner. These lighter planes take off faster and smoother."

Carly continued to watch as the details of roads and buildings became smaller and eventually faded away as they soared up into the clouds. They watched a comedy show on the TV while holding hands, until the plane leveled off and the captain announced it was safe to move around the cabin.

He turned toward her with a smile and twinkle in his blue eyes. "Would you like the grand tour now, *ma chérie?*"

"I would love to."

He took her hand and led her past the divider and she saw the table with room for four that she'd caught a glimpse of earlier. "This is the dining area. Lunch will be served in about an hour, but there are snacks and drinks in here." He opened a small fridge under the countertop with a variety of drinks, pudding, Jell-O, cheese, fruit cups, and veggies with dip. Then he opened a thin pantry with candy, pretzels, chips, and beef jerky.

"There's about every snack you could possibly want in here. How do you keep from gaining a thousand pounds when you travel?"

He chuckled and rubbed his toned stomach, pretending to push it out like he'd eaten too much. "Self-control?" She swatted his arm playfully before he went on. "No, I normally don't have this many choices of snacks on the jet, unless I'm traveling with a guest. I wasn't sure what you would like, so I had it stocked with a variety of things."

"Well, thank you," she said, pausing to kiss him on the cheek. "Hopefully I will be able to show the same self-control you do. Those chocolate bars look delicious."

They shared a laugh before Carly looked above the counter, observing plates, cutlery, and wine glasses stored in the glass cabinet. There was also a sound system and adjustable lighting controlled by a touch screen on the wall that kept her entertained for a few minutes. After she took it all in, he led her past another divider. "Now, this is my favorite room. The lounge slash movie room."

Carly looked around in amazement, seeing a leather couch with pillows and cup holders on the arm rests. Across from it was a large flatscreen television with surround sound and an entertainment center underneath. She saw a variety of movies and games through the glass. "Wow, this plane is like a five-star hotel with wings!"

He nodded with an amused lift of his eyebrow. "Yes, believe it or not, it even has a small bedroom and shower in the back. I rarely use it though, unless I have an overnight flight. However, if you get tired, feel free to take a nap back there. It has room darkening shades and sound proofing so you won't be disturbed."

"Oh, thank you, but I couldn't think of sleeping during a trip like this. This is all too exciting and I don't want to miss anything."

He showed her a few more features of the plane, including a brief look at the bedroom and a larger lavatory. Then they headed back into the lounge. He motioned toward the couch. "Would you like to sit and play a game before lunch? Maybe a few rounds of rummy?"

Carly nodded, eyeing the couch. "That sounds great, but won't we need a table?"

He nodded. "I've got that all worked out." Carly watched as he pulled up the center couch cushion and slide an expandable table out. "Voila!" he exclaimed, folding down the sides until it became a flat surface.

She let out a giggle at his enthusiasm. "That's amazing. This jet has so many hidden surprises."

"Just wait until we arrive in Paris. I have plenty more surprises up my sleeve." He retrieved a deck of cards from the entertainment center and returned to the couch with them.

She arched an amused eyebrow. "You're actually shuffling those by hand? I figured you'd have some ingenious automatic card shuffler to do that."

He grinned while sliding the cards from the box. "No, *mon amour*. Some things are better done the old fashioned way."

Carly's heart raced as she watched him shuffle the cards. There he was again, calling her 'my love' in French. Would she ever build up the courage to say it back to him?

For lunch, Luc wanted to give Carly a taste of French food before they arrived in Paris. He had arranged in advance for *croque monsieur* to be served, a delicious fancied up version of a toasted ham and cheese sandwich and *soupe à l'oignon*, a kind of

French onion soup with croutons and cheese melted on the top. To top it off, they enjoyed delicious chocolate soufflés.

She held her stomach after taking one last bite of the rich dessert. "Well, I definitely can't eat like this every day while we're in Paris. I'll have gained ten pounds by the time we get back."

"And you'll still be drop dead gorgeous."

"You're hopeless," she scoffed with an adorable goofy grin on her face.

His eyebrow arched, amused by her reaction. "Maybe so, but this is your first trip to Europe and you should enjoy yourself. There's no use worrying about calories during an adventure like this, *oui?*"

Carly nodded with a grin. "*Oui.*"

"Good." Luc sighed and leaned back in his chair. "Would you like to watch a movie or two while our food settles?"

She nodded. "Yes, I'd like that very much."

Luc led Carly back to the lounge and watched as she looked through the movie options. She set out a few possibilities before gasping in excitement. "You have *The Princess Bride!*" She took the case out and hugged it close. "Would you mind if we watched it? I'll let you pick out the next one."

He chuckled, loving her enthusiasm. "Of course, we can watch it. I wouldn't mind at all. It's one of my favorites, actually."

"It is?"

Luc nodded and busied himself closing the blinds and the dividers to watch the movie. "Yes, my mother convinced me to give it a chance, and I enjoyed it so much, we started watching it together all the time."

Carly grinned while taking the movie out of the case and placing it into the DVD player. "I always knew I liked your mom."

"And she likes you, too." They sat on the couch together with

Carly cuddled close to him. He wrapped his arms around her, savoring the way she fit into his embrace.

They watched the movie together, laughing at the funny parts and reciting movie lines they'd memorized. Joy filled his heart, realizing how well-matched they were. They had similar sense of humor and shared many of the same interests, yet in some ways they were complete opposites. Luc knew both their similarities and even their differences were what made them so compatible.

After finishing the movie, they decided on a second one. Carly cuddled up to him again, but about half an hour later, her head grew heavy against his chest. He smiled and kissed the top of her head, remembering what she'd said earlier about not wanting to fall asleep and miss something about their trip. It turned out she was tired after all. Even after his arm went numb, Luc didn't mind. It was a privilege to hold and protect her in his arms while she slept—a privilege he treasured.

## 21

Carly watched in anticipation as the lights of Paris Charles de Gaulle Airport came into view. Part of her wished she would be able to see all the details of the surrounding city in daylight, but she would have to wait for the next morning for that. It was the middle of the night because of the time difference. Still, just knowing they had arrived in Paris made Carly feel like a shaken-up can of soda, ready to burst.

"Here we are, *ma chérie*," Luc said when they landed. "Your first moment in Europe."

"This is so exciting! Thank you for inviting me along, Luc. I've had an unforgettable trip already." Carly buried her face in his shirt, barely able to suppress a squeal from escaping her mouth.

He wrapped his arm around her and kissed the top of her head. "And thank you for agreeing to come. The trip would have seemed bland without you. I probably would have spent an exorbitant amount of time going over business stuff or reading."

She craned her neck to look up at him with an impish grin. "Sorry I drooled on your shirt earlier when I fell asleep. I didn't think I was tired, but I guess I needed a nap after all. At least I don't talk in my sleep like Kendall. At least I don't think I do."

"I didn't mind," Luc assured with a chuckle. "It's good you were able to sleep for a little while. With the time difference, you'll probably wake up with jetlag tomorrow morning." He peeked at his high-tech watch, which had automatically updated with the time change. "Forgive me. I meant later on *this* morning."

"What time do we have to wake up tomorrow?" She covered her face and corrected herself. "Well, you know what I mean."

"I'll most likely wake up around seven. I have to meet with my father early before his meetings, but you can sleep in until around ten if you'd like. I'll be back by then and we can share a brunch."

"Okay, that sounds good," Carly agreed, although the thought of him leaving her in a foreign hotel caused her heart to race.

He had pulled out a tablet and was busy scrolling through his schedule, not even noticing her apprehension. "You'll have a fitting for your gown around eleven. Then we can spend the rest of the day sightseeing. What do you say?"

She nodded, letting out a deep breath she'd been holding without realizing it. "That sounds perfect. When is the banquet?"

"Saturday afternoon. You'll meet my father that day, too. Unfortunately, he'll be swamped with meetings today. However, there's no doubt my brother will probably pop in out of the blue. He tends to do that. Now, I have to warn you, he's a little bit of a Casanova…as in he flirts with every beautiful woman he sees. I've asked him to be on his best behavior, but if he slips up a time or two, try not to take it to heart. He really does mean well."

"Okay, thanks for the heads up." Carly gulped down a lump in her throat and her shoulders grew tense as the plane taxied to a secluded terminal at the airport. "That reminds me, how do I greet your family? I've seen French people kiss each other on the cheek as a greeting. Am I expected to do that?"

Luc smiled and kissed her hand. "That is typically a greeting reserved for family and close friends, but you will not be expected to do so. A handshake will suffice."

"Good," she said, feeling her shoulders relax again. "I'm glad I asked. I wouldn't want to make an embarrassing mistake."

"You'll do just fine, Carly. The most important thing is to be yourself. Everyone is going to love you."

"Even your father?"

Luc shrugged. "Even if he doesn't approve at first, he will in time…especially when he sees how happy I am with you."

A smile curved on Carly's lips as she met his sincere gaze. She'd never met a man who made her feel more beautiful, loved, and treasured. "Luc, there's something I've been meaning to tell you."

He nodded for her to go on, but at the same time the pilot turned off the seatbelt sign and announced their arrival. The moment interrupted, they both concentrated on collecting their small carry-on bags and exiting the aircraft. As they descended the steps to the tarmac, there was a limo waiting for them and two bodyguards standing close by to accompany them. It was different at first, not being alone, but Carly quickly forgot they were there as Luc pointed out landmarks along the way to the hotel. As they drove past the Eifel tower and the Louvre Museum, he sighed. "I'm sorry. Everything will be much easier to see in the daylight."

She leaned into his embrace while continuing to watch out the window. "Don't apologize. Seeing the city like this at night with all the lights is amazing. When I see it tomorrow it will be like a completely different world. I'll be seeing it through new eyes."

When they arrived at the hotel, Carly looked up in awe at the elegant architecture. The high arches and chandeliers seemed to descend from the heavens. She held Luc's hand as he led her to the elevator with the bodyguards accompanying them. Along the way, she noticed a few hotel guests who were up at a late hour gawking, but the attention was the furthest thing from her mind at the moment. Nothing could distract her from the special moments she shared with Luc that evening.

They took the elevator to the top level and he led her into the first room to the left. "This will be your suite and mine is next door."

Carly observed the features of the luxurious suite, hardly able to breathe. They entered and walked through a formal sitting room with a fireplace, vaulted ceiling with a crystal chandelier, and elegant pillars leading to the next room. The walls were adorned with French paintings and the open tulle curtains revealed a stunning view of the Eiffel Tower.

Luc grinned at her as she took it all in. "This is just part of it." He motioned for her to go on without him. "Go have a look around. Let me know if the suite will be adequate for you."

"Adequate?" she said with a chuckle. "This one space is twice as big as my bedroom!" She crossed through the next arched doorway, revealing a large living space, complete with a large screen television and furniture. The walls had built-in shelves with a variety of books, movies and music—more than she could ever hope to enjoy during her stay in Paris.

When she walked into the bedroom, Carly squealed and leapt onto the king-sized four poster bed, stacked with enough plush lacy pillows to swallow her. She sunk into the heavenly down comforter and looked up at the elegant tulle draped over the bed. After the long plane ride, she could have fallen asleep instantly.

"Is everything all right in there?" Luc called from the sitting room.

She released a breathless laugh. "Yes, everything is perfect!

Just let me have a look at the bathroom." She forced herself up and checked out the bathroom, squealing with delight again. "A walk-in closet and a jacuzzi tub? This is a girl's dream hotel room!" She walked back out to meet Luc, smiling so big her cheeks began to ache. "Yep, I'd say the suite will do. Next time I might prefer one with a tad bit more room or maybe my own swimming pool."

He laughed at her snarky remark and pulled her in for a kiss. Carly lingered in Luc's arms as he traced the curve of her cheek with his fingers. "I'm glad you like it, *ma chérie*. I should go for the evening so we both can get some rest."

"Rest? How could I ever rest after all the exciting things I've experienced today?"

He pulled her close again, planting a tender kiss on her forehead. "Promise me you'll try? I have a busy day, full of adventures planned for us tomorrow."

She nodded. "I promise."

"Good." He backed away slowly, holding onto her hand until she could no longer reach. *"Bonne nuit, mon amour."*

Carly watched him leave before approaching the door to latch it for the night. She leaned her back against it with a contented sigh. The suite was amazing, but the best part was being with Luc in one of the most romantic cities in the world. She'd made a promise to Luc she would try to sleep, but could she keep it when she had so many wonderful things to look forward to in the morning?

Luc woke up at seven on the dot. In spite of only getting a few hours of sleep, he felt energized and ready to start the day. It was no surprise since he was typically wired on most of his business trips. The first day home afterwards was usually the day he crashed and his secretary knew not to schedule any appointments then, unless they were urgent. Luc prepared for the day, ate a small bowl of oatmeal, and grabbed his insulated mug of coffee before heading out the door.

He left the back way with his guards to avoid the media who would have inevitably known of his arrival and swarmed him otherwise. The limo awaited in the underground parking area and took him the short distance to his father's estate. When Luc arrived, he headed up to his father's rooms on the second floor. When he entered his father's study, he was sitting at the desk, looking over some documents. To his surprise, he was still in his pajamas and robe. It wasn't like him not to be ready for the day yet, especially with all the meetings planned for the day.

"Luc, it's wonderful to see you," his father said in French when he entered, the language he preferred to converse in. He stood with a groan and held his abdomen with one hand, bracing his free one on the desk to help him stand.

"Good morning, Father." Luc approached and they kissed each other's cheeks.

"I trust you had a good flight?"

"Yes, we did." When he had a chance to study his father's pale, gaunt face, hunched stature, and lightly yellowed eyes, his brows furrowed. "Are you not feeling well?"

He sputtered out a few coughs, but smiled and patted Luc's shoulder. "I'm as well as can be expected. There is no need to concern yourself with my health. There are more important matters to worry about right now."

They sat across the desk from each other. "Will you be attending the meetings today? I thought your work day started at eight?"

He nodded. "Oh, yes. It does, but your brother has recently persuaded me to use video conferencing. It saves me from having to walk so much. I saved my most important meetings for the afternoon and will attend those in person."

Luc raised an eyebrow and chuckled. "So, Pierre convinced

you of something I've been trying to for years? Regardless, I'm glad. You've been under too much stress. It's time to take better care of yourself."

His father nodded before waving away his concern. "Enough about my health. Did your *American* girlfriend come with you as planned?"

Luc nodded, the fact his father's words lingered around "American" not passing his notice "Yes, Carly's here. I hope you'll still feel up to having lunch with us tomorrow afternoon. I would like for you to meet her before the banquet."

"Since you insist."

He leaned back in his chair with a sigh. Luc had been expecting some resistance, but deep down, he wished his father would show a fraction of interest in learning more about the woman he'd grown to love. "I think you'll really like her. She's intelligent, creative, and outspoken...not to mention beautiful."

"Yes," his father agreed with a flourish of his hand before turning to his computer and typing something. "As you've mentioned over the phone. I'm sorry, son, but I can't help thinking this woman is the reason you are so reluctant to take on your responsibilities here. What happens when she decides she's done being in the public eye and leaves you? Are you willing to trade your family and inheritance for just a few short months with this American?"

Luc clenched his jaw, not liking how the blunt words had flowed from his father's mouth so easily. "Carly is only one of my reasons." He paused to calm himself and asked God for the right words before continuing. "I'm sorry, Father, but after careful thought and prayer, I will not be moving to Paris. Elnora is my home, and I have had success with the hotels the company has built in the States. I don't want to leave them under the leadership of someone else. Not when I worked so hard to establish them."

His father's blue eyes flamed at him. "In other words, you're abandoning your responsibilities and family when they need you the most."

Luc closed his eyes for a moment and released a deep sigh. There was no point in lashing back at his father. He was worried about the future of his company and legacy as any successful businessman would. Luc understood that. "I would still like to be involved as much as possible. I would gladly work from my home base to do so, and travel to Paris quarterly if need be to make sure everything is running smoothly."

His father muttered something in French under his breath and waved him away. "I have meetings to prepare for. We will talk more about this later."

Luc stared at his father for a few seconds, bewildered. What life experience had made the man so bitter and shut off, even from his own family? He wasn't sure if the conversation could have gone any worse, but it was too late to try and rephrase things now or explain his reasoning for not wanting to move to Paris any further. Luc stood to walk out, resigning himself to the idea his father may never accept his decision. Regardless, he would not waver.

## 22

Carly slowly came to consciousness, a dream of traveling to Paris with Luc ebbing in her memory. She saw flashes of a romantic plane ride and the lights of the Eiffel Tower through the window of the limo. When she woke up and blinked a few times, the tulle above her bed and the elegant vaulted ceiling of her suite came into focus, and the blissful realization slowly unfurled in her mind. It wasn't a dream at all. Carly grinned from ear to ear while glancing at her phone on the nightstand. It was a little past nine and Luc would be returning to have brunch about ten.

She padded into the spacious bathroom and wondered where to start. There was the jacuzzi tub, but Carly didn't want to risk that at the moment. If she sank into a luxurious, warm, bubbling bath, she'd want to spend an hour soaking, and there wasn't time for that. Instead she wasted about ten minutes fiddling with the touch screen settings in the huge walk in shower. Eventually she settled on some classical music and the rain setting. She spent another fifteen enjoying the feeling of the soothing warm water coming directly from the ceiling. It was amazing how it seemed to come from nowhere. Afterwards, she found a soft robe and settled by the window with a cup of coffee to gaze at the amazing view of the Eiffel Tower while allowing her hair to air-dry for a few minutes. It was so peaceful and serene, Carly lost track of time, until her phone buzzed.

I'M BACK. READY FOR BRUNCH?

Carly gasped, seeing it was five past ten. She was nowhere near ready, but texted back anyway. ALMOST. GIVE ME FIVE.

Carly leapt out of her chair and concentrated on drying her hair and brushing her teeth first. Then she found a casual oversized shirt and leggings in her bag. After hearing a light knock, she groaned while walking to the door and opening it. Had he ever seen her without makeup before? Maybe when the rain washed it all off during their first date at the vineyard. Still, it was enough to give her anxiety. She had blonde eyebrows that seemed almost nonexistent unless she darkened them with eyebrow liner.

Luc came in and handed her a bouquet of flowers in a vase before kissing her. "*Bonjour, ma chérie.* I have to say, you are the most beautiful sight I've seen this morning."

She scoffed lightly while placing the bouquet in the center of the table, trying to avoid his eyes. "Are you sure? I lost track of time and haven't even had a chance to pencil in my eyebrows or put on mascara yet."

He pulled her into his arms again, caressing her cheek with his fingers. "Don't feel like you have to wear makeup on my account. Your natural face is even more beautiful to me, Carly."

Her heart fluttered as she gazed into his sincere blue eyes, realizing he wasn't saying it just to make her feel better. Luc meant every word. He leaned in to kiss her when there was another knock on the door. "Well, our brunch has arrived. I hope you're hungry." Carly nodded and watched him walk over to let the server in.

Breakfast was delicious with a variety of dishes, including crepes with fruit topping, French toast, eggs, sausage, croissants, and a variety of other things. Carly hadn't realized how hungry she was until she started eating. She indulged, sampling a little bit of everything. It wasn't until halfway through the meal she realized Luc had barely touched his food. She looked into his eyes with concern. "Is everything all right?"

He nodded and managed a smile. "Yes, I'm just not that hungry. I had a small bowl of oatmeal this morning."

Carly studied him for a second, somehow knowing he wasn't being entirely truthful. She topped one of the crepes with some of the cream cheese mixture and glanced back up at him as he gazed out the window toward the Eiffel Tower in the distance. "I take it the meeting with your father didn't go as you hoped?"

Luc sighed and turned his face toward her again. "You can already read me like a book, Carly. I didn't want to worry you with it, but I guess you should know the truth. He isn't happy with my decision not to move to Paris. He doesn't look very well either, which makes it even harder to negotiate with him. I don't want to cause him any undue stress."

Carly nodded. "I understand. I'm sorry this is so difficult for you. Is there anything I can do to help?"

A smile spread across his face as he reached for her hand. "Just you being here is help enough. Your presence gives me courage to stand my ground."

"Well, good. I'm happy to be there for you in any way I can."

"Thank you." He lounged back in his chair, the stress in his eyes fading away. "So, after you're done with your fitting, you'll want to dress in something business casual for our day out. I have somewhere very special I'd like to take you first."

Carly's heart raced as she reached for a spoonful of fruit for her crepe. "Where are we going?"

Luc gave her a playful grin. "That, *mon amour*, is a secret."

The fitting was a little more invasive than Carly imagined. The designer and seamstress had fluttered into the room at eleven on the dot with tape measures, pins, scissors and her half-finished sapphire gown. It was a flowing, asymmetrical style with one shoulder and fabric flowers sewn along the top angle of the bodice and ruffles after the waist. She stood in high heels on a pedestal patiently for almost a full hour as the two women jabbered on and on in French while measuring, pinning, and snipping.

Finally, when Carly's feet started to throb, the seamstress secured one more pin and the designer stepped back with a proud smile and clasped her hands together. *"Voila...Magnifique!"*

Carly breathed a sigh of relief after they helped her out of the gown and into a robe. It was a small miracle she'd managed to escape from it without getting skewered like a kabob from all the pins. After they left, she fixed her hair and makeup before changing into her favorite knee length red dress, paired with leggings, suede ankle boots, and a matching scarf. When she was finished getting ready, she went downstairs to meet Luc in the lobby for their sightseeing date.

When she spotted Luc in one of the leather chairs on the main level, he put down a book he'd been reading and removed his glasses, standing to meet her. "Wow, you look amazing, Carly."

She gave him a shy grin, taking in his dark red sweater with a collared shirt underneath, matched with a tweed jacket and jeans. "You don't look so bad yourself, Monsieur Belshaw. And our brains are in sync today. Somehow we both wore red."

He grinned, taking her hand in his. "I guess so."

They left out a back entrance to a parking garage where Luc's limo was waiting. Once they were seated, Luck took out a blindfold. "Here, you'll have to wear this before we leave the garage."

Carly let out a nervous chuckle while leaning closer so he could tie on the blindfold. "What are you up to?"

"I can't tell you," he said, while securing the knot. "It will ruin the surprise."

"Okay, I promise I'll try not to peek."

Luc wrapped his arm around her and Carly cuddled close to him during the ten-minute drive to who knew where. Even if Luc hadn't blindfolded her, she wouldn't have had a clue where they were going anyway. She knew very little about the landmarks in Paris, but she played along. Every date with Luc was an adventure and she was determined to enjoy every second of this one. When the limo stopped, Luc led her out of the limo and held her hand.

They walked down what she assumed was a sidewalk and then turned. She heard doors opening. "*Bienvenue*, Monsieur Belshaw," a man said.

"*Merci*," Luc responded and led Carly forward again. "There is a flight of stairs ahead of you," he said before helping her navigate them.

The air became warmer and once they reached the top of the stairs he stopped and removed her blindfold. Carly squinted in the light, but when her eyes adjusted, she saw they were standing in the middle of an elegant oval room with familiar paintings displayed on the wall.

"Welcome to the *Musée Marmottan Monet*."

Carly stifled a gasp with both hands. After the shock wore off, she wrapped her arms around Luc and kissed his cheek. "This is amazing! I can't believe we're here."

A wide grin spread across his face. "I hoped you'd love it. I reserved an hour for a private tour of the museum."

"Thank you, Luc. It's the best surprise you could have planned for me."

They walked around the museum together, holding hands and taking their time to study each Monet painting. When they reached the famous painting, "Impression Sunrise," she saw Luc's eyes light up. "It's amazing to think this is the original. I can just imagine him racing up a ridge by the sea with his supplies, trying to capture the variations of light before they changed."

Carly nodded, heart racing at the thought. "I bet he never would have dreamed his work would be so famous one day."

Luc's eyes remained focused on the paint strokes, so blue and intense they almost matched some of the blue in the waves. "At the time, the fame wasn't important. Like any passionate artist, painting wasn't just a job or hobby for him. It was a necessity. Life has no meaning for an artist who's not creating… no matter what form of art it might be."

"Is that how you felt when you didn't paint for two years?"

Luc turned to her with a thoughtful expression. "Yes. Although I didn't realize how colorless and dull my world had become until God brought you into my life, Carly. He helped me realize there was still light in the world, even after I'd shut it out of my life for so long. Like the sun rising after the dawn in this painting, revealing the colors of the sea, pier, and ships. I'd been starving myself for so long, and when I finally picked up a brush again, I felt my hunger to live and paint return. Part of my inspiration came from Angeline, but I was wrong to think *all* of it did. My true inspiration comes from God and His creation."

Carly moved closer, wrapping her arm around him. "I'm glad your inspiration returned, Luc…and that I've been around to witness it."

"Me too."

She leaned her head against his chest, releasing a contented sigh. They'd shared so much together in the short time they'd known each other. Carly felt all her doubts and apprehension fading away as they continued to gaze at the painting. None of the obstacles she'd worried about in the past mattered anymore. As long as Luc stayed in the US, they could build a life together.

She wanted it so badly, she thought her heart would burst. After they finished looking at the artwork in the room, they moved onto the next. Carly's heart pounded as her fingers tightened around Luc's. "You know, I've been practicing my French for when I meet your family tomorrow and for the banquet...but there are certain phrases I'm still struggling with. It makes me nervous I'll say something wrong."

"They won't expect you to say everything perfectly." Luc smiled at her as they stopped by a group of Monet paintings of waterlilies. "It can be difficult to learn a new language. How about you say a phrase out loud to me and I'll see how your pronunciation is?"

"Okay," Carly said and thought for a moment before saying the phrase she'd been practicing. *"Je t'aime plus chaque jour."*

"You said, 'I love you more each day.' That was almost perfect, except plus should be pronounced like pree-ch, like this." He repeated the phrase correctly and had her repeat it again. Then he smiled at her. "Perfect! But it doesn't seem like a phrase you'd use to meet new people though."

She grinned and took both Luc's hands in hers. "Here, let me try another one." She took a deep breath and said another phrase. *"Je suis fou de toi,* Luc."

He laughed. "Now you said, 'I'm crazy about you.' The pronunciation was flawless that time. I'm impressed you've learned so fast, but who are you planning on saying this to?"

Carly released a flustered laugh. "I'll try one more time." She gazed into his cobalt eyes and gulped down a lump in her throat, praying he'd understand. *"Je t'aime de tout mon cœur,* Luc."

"I love you with all my heart, Luc," he translated and his eyes finally filled with understanding. "You love me?"

She nodded, smiling through happy tears. *"Oui, je t'aime beaucoup."*

A smile bloomed on his lips before he pulled her into his

embrace and kissed her so passionately, she felt dizzy. "I love you too, Carly, with all my heart."

"I'm sorry it took me so long to say it."

He pulled her closer, resting his cheek against the top of her head. "I thought I knew what was in your heart, but I knew you'd say it when you were ready...and at just the right moment. It was well worth the wait, *mon amour*."

# 23

The next day, it was no surprise to Luc his father canceled the brunch he had planned, but he tried not to let it ruin Carly's first trip to Paris. Yesterday had been a dream come true. After their tour at the museum, they enjoyed a light lunch at his favorite little café before seeing the Eiffel Tower up close and touring the Notre Dame Cathedral. They topped the day off with a private dinner cruise on the Seine. Luc wanted to take her to Giverny to see Monet's historic home and gardens where he'd painted the famous bridge and water lily scenes, but that would have to wait until Monday.

They had a low-key breakfast at the hotel and spent the morning watching a movie together before his brother called. Luc went into the other room to answer it. "Good morning, little brother. I've been here a whole day and a half and it surprises me I haven't seen you yet."

Pierre chuckled on the other end of the line. "I'm sorry. Celine and I had other plans yesterday. I wanted to come see you in the morning yesterday, but it just didn't work out."

Luc smiled. "That's all right. When do I get the chance to meet the beautiful Celine you seem so enamored with?"

"You can meet her now, if you want to. She'll be here at Chateau de Belshaw for the next hour. Father wanted you to come here anyway. He said a family meeting is in order...or something to that effect."

Luc sighed and pinched the bridge of his nose. "He canceled the brunch where he was supposed to meet Carly. Now he wants me to come to a family meeting?"

"I know, I know. He's a hard person to understand sometimes." Pierre released a weary sigh. "Could you please just come? This is important, but I can't explain why. He asked me not to."

"Sure," Luc responded, bracing his arm against the wall. "I'll be there within the hour."

After Pierre hung up, Luc looked through the thin book of numbers at the hotel and made a few calls before going back into the living room to speak with Carly. He hoped she wouldn't be too disappointed he had to leave.

She paused the movie and looked up when he came in. "Is everything all right?"

Luc nodded and managed an unconvincing smile. "Yes, but I have to go to my father's for a few hours."

"Do you want me to come along?" Carly started to get up, but he sat down with her instead. It was clear from her gaze—she knew something was up. "No, I don't think that would be a good idea right now. My father has something to tell me and I have a feeling it's not good news."

She reached for his hand with a frown. "I'm sorry, Luc. I'll be praying."

He sighed, squeezing her hand. "Thank you. Now, since I have to go, I don't want you to be sitting here in this room. I signed you up for some spa treatments downstairs after lunch. They offer about anything you could think of, so enjoy yourself and don't look at the prices."

A huge grin spread across her face as she leaned forward to

hug him. "Why are you so sweet to me?"

He grinned and kissed her. "I think the answer is quite obvious. I love you." He let her go and started to stand from the couch. "Now just remember to be back upstairs by four. The designer will be here to deliver your dress and the hairdresser soon after. I should be back by then, too. We'll ride to the Louvre together."

She nodded and blew him a kiss. "I promise to be ready on time. See you soon."

Luc said goodbye and fifteen minutes later, he was greeted with a warm hug from his brother at his father's home. "Thank you for coming."

He smiled at Pierre, glad to see he was happy and well. "It's good to be here."

Pierre motioned toward the beautiful raven-haired woman beside him with a twinkle in his blue eyes. "I would like to introduce you to my wife, Celine."

"Wife?" Luc sputtered out a surprised laugh. "I had a feeling you were going to have some big news. I thought you'd say you were engaged. Congratulations!"

"Thank you, brother."

He moved to shake Celine's hand but she hugged him instead. "It's nice to finally meet you. Pierre has told me so much about you."

"The same. So, when did this all happen?"

"A few days ago," Pierre spoke up while pulling Celine into his embrace. "We eloped and spent a few days in Venice for a mini honeymoon. We came back yesterday."

"Well, no wonder you were too busy to come see us yesterday." He shook his head in amazement. "You finally decided to settle down and start a family. I'm happy for you."

His brother smiled even bigger and he kissed his wife's cheek. "I guess when you finally meet the right one, you don't want to wait to delay making a commitment any longer. It was clear within the first few weeks Celine was the one I wanted to spend my life with. Life is short."

Pierre shared a look with Celine that sent shivers through Luc. What had he meant by that last sentence? "So, should we go visit with Father now?"

His brother nodded and hugged Celine one last time before she said her goodbyes. When she was gone, Pierre patted his shoulder. "Before we go in, I wanted to warn you. What he has to say might come as a shock, but I think I may have a remedy that will help ease the situation."

The afternoon flew by as Carly enjoyed a massage, mani-pedi, face mask, and several other spa treatments. She finished a Christian historical romance she'd borrowed from the hotel room and felt so relaxed she could float away on a cloud. It wasn't until a timer went off on her phone that she realized it was time to head back upstairs to change into her dress and have her hair done. Thank goodness she remembered to set one.

Carly thanked the ladies at the hotel spa and made it back to her room in time to meet the dress designer and hair dresser. Within an hour she was almost ready. She stood in front of the floor-length mirror in the walk-in closet, finishing her make up before stepping back to study her reflection. The gown was modest to her relief, but elegant and perfectly tailored to complement her every curve. She couldn't wait for Luc to see her. Where was he anyway? She checked her phone, surprised to see he was late. Carly started to call him when there was a knock on the door.

One of the hotel attendants was at the door with a large velvet jewelry box tied with a bow. "*Monsieur* wanted me to give you this to wear tonight and let you know he has been delayed.

He will now be meeting you at the Louvre. Your limo is waiting whenever you are ready, *mademoiselle*."

"*Merci*," Carly said before taking the box and closing the door again. It was disappointing Luc couldn't ride with her to the banquet like they'd planned, but she was sure he had a good reason for not returning. She opened the box, gasping when she saw a diamond and sapphire necklace with a matching bracelet and earrings set in white gold. Carly put them on quickly before hurrying out the door. Two bodyguards were waiting to escort her to the limo.

She felt like royalty while on the way to the Louvre Palace where many kings and queens had stayed in the past. When the limo stopped, Carly spotted Luc right away, waiting for her by a triangular shaped fountain in his tuxedo.

"You're a vision, Carly," Luc said when she approached.

Heat tingled in her cheeks as she looked down at her dress, enjoying the way it shimmered in the lights from the Louvre. "Thank you."

"Sorry I couldn't meet you at the hotel like we planned. Something came up with my father." His eyes darkened for only a moment, but she saw right through the wall he was trying to hold up.

"Is he all right?"

"That's a long story…" he started to explain but they were interrupted by a sea of media snapping pictures and trying to ask them questions. He offered them a polite wave and prompted her to pose next to him for a quick photo before escorting her to the safety of the *Pyramide du Louvre*.

Carly couldn't help marveling at the hundreds of panes of glass making up the large pyramid structure as they sparkled in the evening sky, surrounded by the historical palace. It was a unique and stunning mix of historic and modern architecture. Carly found herself wishing she had a canvas and paints to capture the scene. A silver and gold theme on the tables and banners made the entire space shine like a pirate's box of treasure.

For about thirty minutes, they made their rounds and Luc introduced her to delegates from all over Europe. She could speak simple phrases to the ones who spoke French and a few from America and the UK spoke English, but mostly, she did a lot of nodding and smiling—so much her cheeks ached.

"You're doing very well," Luc whispered in her ear after introducing her to a German businessman and his wife.

Soon after, they were greeted by a tall blond man with cobalt blue eyes like Luc and a woman with shimmering raven hair and hazel eyes. "Carly, I'd like to introduce you to my brother, Pierre, and his new wife, Celine."

She smiled in recognition and shook both their hands, speaking in English since Luc had. "It's a pleasure to finally meet you both."

Pierre kept her hand for a moment and kissed it. "*Le plaisir est à moi, mademoiselle.* Luc has talked about you almost non-stop all afternoon."

She let out a nervous laugh, realizing what Luc meant about him being a Casanova. Pierre was full of charm and swagger. However, she was relieved he spoke mostly in English for her benefit. "I hope all good things?"

Luc's brother smiled. "*Oui*, of course. I'm happy he has found someone special like you." He motioned toward the front of the venue. "Come, seats are reserved for both of you at the front table. Carly, you may sit next to Celine so you can become better acquainted."

She smiled at Celine walking next to her. The tall, sophisticated French model smiled back but Carly couldn't help feeling a little intimidated by her. When they made it to the reserved table, Luc and Pierre pulled out chairs for them. They sat for a few minutes enjoying some hors d'oeuvres before Pierre stood and told Luc something in French she couldn't understand.

He nodded to his brother before turning to kiss Carly's cheek. "That's our cue. We have to go find our father and sit on the platform with him for the presentations. I'll see you afterwards."

Carly nodded and watched him walk away with his brother. While waiting for the presentations to start, she made small talk with Celine, but she knew very little English and Carly was limited in her French, so they stuck to simple phrases and some hand motions.

About ten minutes later, an orchestra by the platform cued up and performed a beautiful piece. Soon after, Mr. Belshaw Senior took the stage with Luc and Pierre following close behind. Her heart thumped with pride, seeing Luc up there, looking like the powerful and talented leader he was. Not only that, but he showed so much care for his loved ones, even difficult ones like his father. Carly realized anew what a gem he really was.

She didn't expect to understand most of the speeches in French, but was pleasantly surprised when some translators stood to the side of the platform with microphones. She was able to listen to the English speaking one with ease. When Luc's father stood up, he needed Luc and Pierre to stand on either side of him to help him to the podium. As he spoke about his vision for the future of the company, she listened intently, amazed at how much he resembled Luc. They had similar mannerisms, too.

"This company has been in my family for generations," he continued speaking. "I have watched it grow exponentially in my lifetime. While it is difficult to think of changes in tradition, changes are inevitable. With that said, I have an important decision to announce. My son, Luc, is officially stepping up to be the new CEO of Belshaw Enterprises…"

The rest of his speech faded into the background as Carly processed what Mr. Belshaw had said. Luc would become CEO, meaning he would have to remain in Paris. She felt the walls of the glass pyramid closing in on her and suddenly she couldn't breathe. Carly's eyes darted around, noticing her table was conveniently close to the exit. "Sorry, I need some fresh air," she whispered to Celine before gathering the train of her gown and escaping outside.

Carly reached the triangular fountain and leaned against it, trying to catch her breath, but the media saw her and started closing in. The space was still too small—the whole city of Paris was closing in to suffocate her with each breath. Somehow, she had to escape it. She had to go home where things made sense.

"Carly," Luc's voice called from behind her as she tried to flee toward the road to hail a cab down. "Wait."

She didn't stop until reaching the busy street, noticing Luc coming up behind her with his bodyguards struggling to catch up. "I...I need some time to think. Please, just leave me alone."

Luc leaned down to take a few deep breaths from running. "You don't understand. It's not what you think. You didn't listen to the rest of the speech."

Tears streamed down her face as she turned to look at him. "You're moving to Paris. I understand that part. And that's okay, Luc. You have responsibilities that were there long before I came along. It would be selfish of me to ask you to abandon them. Please, go back inside to the banquet. It's where you belong. Don't let me keep you from enjoying your new status in the company."

He moved closer and took her hand in his. "Carly, I'm not moving to Paris. I told you that before."

She blinked hard, trying to keep her bottom lip from trembling. "You're not?"

"No, I'm coming back to Elnora with you...well...eventually." He turned to observe his bodyguards keeping the media back. "Can we go somewhere with a little more privacy?"

Carly nodded, still wiping tears as he led her to a large

secluded doorway to the palace. Once they were away from the media, the bodyguards stood post nearby. "I still don't get it. Your father said you stepped into the role of CEO."

He nodded, looking down at his shoes to avoid her eyes for a few seconds. "I did because I have to."

"Have to?"

When he looked up, his eyes were brimming with tears. "My father isn't just sick. He's dying. I just found out this morning." His voice cracked. "I wanted to tell you before the banquet…but I couldn't find the words or time to do it." Luc raked his fingers through his hair, looking so distraught, Carly's heart broke for him.

"Luc, I'm so sorry." She wrapped her arms around him as his body shook with silent sobs.

After a minute, he calmed and wiped his tears. "I'm glad you're here."

"Me too."

He nodded. "I have to stay in Paris for a while to spend time with my father and until the company stabilizes under my new leadership. Then I'll come home to Elnora and run the company from there. Pierre has agreed to work with me on this. He'll take care of immediate business in Paris and I'll visit quarterly." Luc gazed into her eyes, the pain so deep it sent tears rolling down her cheeks. "I don't know how long I'll be here, Carly. It could be months before we're together again."

She moved close to him again, cupping his cheek in her palm, wiping a stray tear with her thumb. "Don't worry about that. Take as much time as you need. I'll be waiting for you, just like you waited for me, my Elnora Monet."

He smiled through his tears and pulled her in for a passionate kiss. "And I'll be thinking of you every day until I return, *mon amour*."

## 24

A month and a half passed by like a sloth for Carly, but gradually she was rewarded with the warmer weather of late spring. She kept in contact with Luc through scattered phone calls, texts, and video chats. It wasn't the same as being with him in person, but Carly knew she had to be patient. Two weeks after returning to Elnora, she heard news Luc's father had passed away. She wanted to go back to Paris to be with Luc, but he urged her to stay home since things were so hectic in the city and the media would be out in full force.

Through the difficult weeks, she kept busy by helping Kendall with the clinic and stopped by the Belshaw Estate twice a week to spend time with Descartes and Athena. The Angora cat had changed drastically from when she first met him, actually meowing and doing figure eights around her ankles, begging for attention. She could hardly wait for Luc to come home and see the transformation. However, as the weeks passed, her mind started playing tricks on her. What if Luc decided to stay in Paris permanently after all?

One Friday, after a long day of walk-in appointments, Carly came home exhausted and started getting out some penne noodles and alfredo sauce for dinner. Her mind swirled with so many questions about her future, she could hardly think straight, but bringing them up to Kendall would be difficult.

"Why don't you relax? I'll take care of the meal tonight," he sister said while reaching into the cabinet for a pot.

"But it's my night to cook. Are you sure?"

Kendall nodded. "Yes, you've been working on overdrive lately. Even I am having trouble keeping up with you."

Carly chuckled and took a seat at the kitchen table. "Didn't realize I was *that* bad."

Kendall scoffed. "What are you trying to say? I know how to relax every once in a while."

"Not since Tyler's been gone. You've been like a machine."

Her sister filled the pot with water and put it on the stove on high heat to boil. "Maybe I should take my own advice, huh?" She settled into the chair adjacent from Carly's and sighed. "Look at us…living on an island and both in love with men all the way across the ocean from us. We might as well be in the dark ages dating pirates."

Carly raised an amused eyebrow. "Yeah, well at least we have better technology."

"You may have a point." They shared a laugh before Kendall sobered. "Are you happy being my assistant, Carly?"

She sat straight up and nodded. "Of course, I am. I love working with you."

Kendall studied her with probing blue eyes. "Now, I want you to be completely honest. I know you enjoy working with me, but is this really the career you want?"

Carly slouched in her chair again, realizing there was no point in trying to hide her true feelings from her sister. "Yes, I thought I wanted it at first. I thought it was the best way to honor Kevin's legacy."

"And now?"

She rested her head in her palm, dreading the uncertainty

her words would bring if she said them out loud. "And now I don't know. Honestly, I spent all that money on classes for a career I really don't enjoy very much, besides the aspect of working with you and the animals we help. I can't stop thinking some other job would fulfill me more."

Carly waited for her sister to be upset with her, but that didn't happen. Instead, when she finally mustered the courage to look up, her sister was smiling. "Then go do it, sis. Go find the job that thrills you into waking up each morning. Take more classes...whatever you need to do."

She stared at Kendall in shock. "And leave you stranded here on Merriweather without an assistant?"

"Alicia is graduating in a few weeks and will be looking for a job. We worked pretty well together while you were gone. Plus, she's from Savannah and only a ferry ride away. I might even be able to convince her to move here. As long as you can stay on and help until she's ready to take over as my assistant."

"Yes, I can do that." Carly launched herself from the seat and hugged her sister with happy tears flowing down her cheeks. "Thank you for understanding."

"You're welcome. If you're happy, I'm happy."

"Oh, I'm too excited to eat now! Would you mind if I went out to Elnora? I want to sit out on Luc's private beach and watch the sunset tonight. Maybe it will give me some ideas."

Kendall laughed. "Sure. Go ahead. Just don't stay out too late. You might get swept away by high tide or snagged by a pirate."

"Argh! Aye aye, Cap'n Kendall," Carly called out before grabbing her purse and rushing out the door.

When she reached the front gate to the mansion the sun had started to lower in the sky and she guessed she had about twenty minutes before it would set. The guard let her in with a friendly *bonjour* and a smile brightening Carly's mood even more. She parked in front of the mansion, but instead of going inside, she headed straight for the walkway through the gardens that led down the ridge to the beach. Sitting in the sand, she removed her flip flops and allowed her toes to sink into the warm surface. It was therapeutic, just like she'd told Luc several months ago.

As the wind tousled her hair, she closed her eyes and started to pray. She thanked God for her family and the time she'd had with her brother before his death. She thanked Him for Luc and asked God to watch over him while they were apart. Last, she asked His leading in what she should do with her life. She knew moving to Merriweather with Kendall hadn't been a mistake. She'd helped Kendall start up her business and didn't regret a single minute of it. She'd also learned so much about herself since moving to the Islands and opened her heart for God to change it. But the question remained...what path was she supposed to go down next?

When Carly opened her eyes, the sunset had barely started to light up the western sky. It was stunning, with shades of magenta, violet, and burnt orange. She wondered why she hadn't thought to bring some paint supplies. With the thought came an idea. It came to her slowly, and then all at once like a rogue wave. With all the mobile businesses starting up around the Islands, why couldn't she start up one of her own? An art studio on wheels where she and Luc could teach lessons wherever they wanted on the Islands. The idea was so ingenious, Carly knew it had to have come directly from above.

Luc woke up on the divan in his studio, disoriented for a moment. Then he felt two warm sleeping cats curled up on his lap and remembered everything. He'd arrived home in the late afternoon, exhausted from his trip, but went to see the cats before taking his nap. Descartes had surprised him with loads of affection upon his arrival, so he stayed in his study petting both cats until passing out on the divan. His trip home was unannounced since he wanted to surprise Carly on Saturday morning.

His blurry eyes drifted to the window, taking in the beautiful sunset. It was enough to will him into full consciousness. Luc gently moved the cats off his lap and hurried around his studio, gathering all the supplies he needed. Soon, he was rushing outside and to the ridge to chase the light before it faded from the sky. Luc had his easel and canvas set up in a matter of seconds. The colors filled up the canvas with ease as he worked with his brush.

After not painting for over a month while in Paris, it was therapeutic to pick up a brush again. Racing to catch the light reminded him how precious life was. He was thankful for the last days he'd spent with his father.

"I'm sorry I wasn't there for you, son," his father had told him a couple of weeks earlier as they sat together on the balcony outside his room at Chateau de Belshaw. "I didn't notice how much time I wasted until it was too late."

Luc patted his father's arm. "It's not too late. We're together now, aren't we?"

He nodded and covered a ragged cough before gazing at the Paris skyline as the sunset painted it a vibrant array of colors. "If I was hard on you in the past, it was because I didn't believe you were living up to your potential." He turned to Luc as a smile gradually formed on his pale lips. "Now I see the man you've become and realize I was wrong. I'm proud of you, and hope this new relationship you're in with the American works out."

"Thank you, Father. Carly makes me happy. She's very special to me."

"Good. Don't make the same mistakes I did and risk dying with so many regrets."

Luc shook his head. "It doesn't have to be like that for you, either. There's still time to make things right. There's even forgiveness and peace if you ask for it. Jesus offers those freely."

His father nodded as his eyes misted over. "It sounds like something worth hearing more about."

Luc thought of the conversation fondly while painting the colors of the sky. A few days after their conversation, his father had given his life to Jesus. It was a bittersweet memory—one he treasured. Luc wiped a few tears on his sleeve before painting the curve of the cove and beach, but something was different about it. Having a private cove, the sight before him was strange. He saw a lone figure sitting there—a woman with her blonde curls flowing in the breeze. Luc fought the urge to call out to the person and ask them what they were doing on private property. Instead, he painted the woman as he saw her—gazing out over the water as the sun faded from the sky. He wasn't sure how she'd gotten there, but he would politely ask her to leave once he completed his artwork.

When Luc was finished, he signed his name like usual, but when he looked up to see if the woman was still there, she had vanished. Luc stood up and approached the path leading down to the water, coming face to face with someone very familiar. "Carly, what are you doing here?"

"I...I should ask you the same question?" she stammered with eyes as wide as sand dollars.

Luc choked out a laugh, realizing it didn't matter at all. He rushed forward and pulled her into his arms, his lips moving over hers passionately as if they hadn't seen each other in years. Her feet dangled as he swung her in a circle.

Carly giggled as he put her back on solid ground, but she remained in his arms, craning her neck to look up at him. "My sister warned me to watch out for pirates, but I never thought I'd be swept off my feet by an island artist."

He grinned and kissed her again. "I came back early. I wanted it to be a surprise."

"Well, it definitely was." They walked over to his easel and she eyed his artwork with a chuckle. "So, I finally made it into one of your paintings without even knowing?"

Luc nodded. "Yes, but you painted your way into my heart several months ago, *mon amour*. Carly, if these past weeks apart have taught me anything, it's how precious life is. I know this is fast, but what about our relationship has been conventional?"

Her blue eyes gazed into his. With the colors of the sunset glowing through her golden hair, she had never looked more beautiful. "What are you trying to say?"

"I don't want to waste a single moment...not when I'm sure of who I want to spend those precious days with." He dropped to one knee and took her hand in his. "Carly Mulligan, will you marry me?"

She covered her face with her free hand before dropping it and nodding with happy tears in her eyes. "Yes, Luc. I'll marry you."

He kissed her hand before standing again to envelop her in his embrace. "I'm sorry. I don't even have a ring yet, but I'll remedy that soon. Want to take a trip to Savannah?"

"Now?"

Luc nodded. "I know a jeweler in town. I could give him a call."

Carly shook her head and reached for a blue rubber band on his easel that had been holding his brushes together. She doubled it over and slipped it onto her finger. "This will be my ring until later. Right now, I don't need anything else. Only my Elnora Monet."

## ACKNOWLEDGMENTS

As always, there are so many people involved in putting a book together and I would like to take a moment to thank them.

First of all, thank you to God for placing this story in my heart. The characters in this book have taught me so much about trusting Him during the storms of life.

Second, thank you for those who helped with the publication process. Thanks to my publisher at Celebrate Lit, Sandy Barela, for making this series possible. I so appreciate the amazing job done by my editor and fellow author in the series, Chautona Havig and my mother Joy Davidson, for helping with proofreading. A special thanks to all the wonderful authors in this series. It has been a joy working with you all so far and your stories are so inspiring to me. Finally, a big shout out to my sister, Jenny Davidson, for taking my author photo. You have such an amazing talent for photography.

Last but not least, thank you to my husband, John, my kids, my extended family, and church family for all your love and support. Also, I'd like to give a shout out to my beta readers, reviewers, and loyal readers waiting patiently for the next book to come out. You all are such an encouragement and I appreciate you.

Blessings.

## ABOUT THE AUTHOR

Rachel Skatvold is a Christian author and homeschooling mom from the Midwest. She enjoys writing inspirational romance and encouraging blogs. Rachel completed her first series, the Riley Family Legacy Novellas in 2014, and is now working on the Hart Ranch Series, set in the Montana wilderness, and the Ladies of Ardena Series, set in medieval times. She is also a contributing author in the Whispers in Wyoming, Brides of Pelican Rapids, and Independence Islands Series. Other than writing, some of her hobbies include singing, reading, and camping in the great outdoors with her husband and two young sons. You can find more information about Rachel and her books on her website: **www.rachelskatvold.com**.

- facebook.com/rachelskatvoldauthor
- twitter.com/rachelskatvold
- bookbub.com/profile/rachel-skatvold

ALSO BY RACHEL SKATVOLD

### Contemporary Romance

**Independence Islands**

Her Merriweather Hero

The Elnora Monet

**Riley Family Legacy**

Beauty Within

Beauty Unveiled

Beauty Restored

**Billionaires and Debutantes**

Chasing a Christmas Carol

### Contemporary Western Romance

**Hart Ranch**

Escaping Reality

Chasing Embers

**Whispers in Wyoming**

Guardian of Her Heart

A Forgetful Heart

Melodies of the Heart

A Searching Heart

Lessons from the Heart

Patient Hearts

## Historical Western Romance

### Brides of Pelican Rapids

Caroline's Quilt

Vivian's Morning Star

## Medieval Romance

### Ladies of Ardena

Lady Airell's Choice

Lady Reagan's Quest

Lady Fiona's Refuge

Lady Gwyneth's Hope

BOOKS IN THE ELNORA ISLAND SERIES

Bookers on the Rocks (Book One) by Chautona Havig
Heart Pressed (Book Two) by Melissa Wardwell
Matchmaker's Best Friend (Book Three) by Kari Trumbo
The Elnora Monet (Book Four) by Rachel Skatvold
Stealing the First Mate (Book Five) by Tabitha Bouldin
Regaining Mercy (Book Six) by Carolyn Miller

# STEALING THE FIRST MATE

## ELNORA ISLAND BOOK FIVE SNEAK PEEK

### TABITHA BOULDIN

# 1

For every great day aboard the *Pirate's Treasure*, there were days capable of making Nigel "Davy" Jones want to hurl his tricorn replica hat into the ocean. After he'd stabbed it with his cutlass and burned the wool contraption to cinders, he would spread its ashes over Mimosa's salty shores. This Saturday morning walked the tightrope between joy and disaster.

Shoving those thoughts into the furthest recesses where they wouldn't frighten customers—especially the little ones—Nigel lowered his towering height to four-year-old levels by squatting on the balls of his feet. Good thing he wasn't a cowboy wearing spurs.

He worked his voice into a tender cadence. "You're certain?"

Blond pigtails bobbed. With a sniffle, his latest reluctant swabbie—aka helper—scrubbed tears from her eyes and hiccupped. "Davy Jones is scary." Her shoulders trembled, followed by a deep sob. "I don't wanna go."

Legs trembling from the pressure of holding the same position, Nigel rocked back until he could sit on the deck and cross his legs. The deck shifted beneath them as the engines chugged, pulling them across open water. Despite the girl's insistence she wanted nothing to do with the pirate boat tour around Independence Islands, they were already aboard and on their way.

He swiped the tricorn off his head and settled it in his lap. The long, purple plume tucked into the hatband danced beneath the girl's chin. She giggled and sniffled. *How do kids do that?*

The crew shouted from behind Nigel, their signal the skit had begun. Nigel waved, indicating they should proceed without him. Captain Black would tell the tale of Reginald Merriweather as they sailed from Mimosa, past Merriweather, and back again. Voices chorused together in song and stomping feet beat a rhythm across the deck. The boards beneath Nigel shivered with the impact of a dozen pairs of boots.

"Can I tell you a secret?" Nigel spun the hat in a slow circle, making the feather dance.

With a nod, the young girl reached out to stroke the feather. Her parents clasped their hands together, fingers flat in prayerful repose, their eyes pleading with him to convince their baby the pirates aboard *Pirate's Treasure* would not throw her to Davy Jones' locker.

*Treasure's* owner, Mr. Riggins, had a No Refund policy that caused parental angst often enough Nigel had an entire spiel prepared for most situations. This though. This was a first. Her insistence that *he* was THE Davy Jones had sucker-punched him. Her fear had been palpable, and his need to fix the world reared its haughty head.

"I'm not a real pirate. My name is Nigel." He held out a hand. Keeping his distance, he allowed the girl to choose whether she would shake his hand. "I'm only pretending. Like in the movies."

Tiny fingers grazed his palm as her gaze jerked up to meet his. "I'm CC."

"Pleasure to meet you, CC." He dropped the tricorn onto her head, and she laughed when her eyes disappeared beneath the brim. "I promise you'll be safe with me...and my friends."

CC sniffed again and palmed his hat from her head. She shoved the brown wool lump onto his head and held out a hand. "Okay."

*That was easy enough.*

Nigel looked up at her parents, silently asking for permission. When they both nodded, Nigel stood and led them toward the group of pirates and tourists laughing and singing around the ship's mast. One couple hooked elbows and whirled around with a raucous, "We've got a tale you'll not believe. A tale of a man who walks the seas!"

A woman's voice drifted down from the crow's nest. Not just any voice. Darcy. The wind ripped her words out to sea before they could be understood, but Nigel could pick Darcy out of the cacophony without fail. He looked up in time to see Darcy swing out of the crow's nest and grasp tightly to the rope ladder. Scrambling down quicker than a monkey, she landed by his side with a thump of her black pirate boots.

CC glanced up, and nothing short of awe could explain her rapt attention. Her voice ticked upward an octave. "There are *girl* pirates?"

Nigel grinned. Apparently, the four other women dancing around the deck hadn't caught CC's attention. He couldn't say he blamed her. Darcy caused the same gape-mouthed expression for him too.

"Are you kidding? We're the best pirates." Darcy patted the blunderbusses strapped crossways over her hips. "No one messes with girl pirates."

Before CC could respond, a loud squawk swamped the shouting and dancing pirates. Captain Black waved his tricorn in a wide arc as his other hand spun the captain's wheel. "Bernie incoming!"

CC's eyes widened and tears once again filled her eyes.

Darcy squatted, bringing herself eye level with the girl. "Aw, don't worry about ole Bernie. He'll land up there with Cap'n."

She winked and pointed at the pelican making lazy circles above the crew. "Watch. Here he goes."

Bernie tucked his wings and glided downward, spinning through the currents like a wobbly top. With another long squawk and an impressive wing flap, Bernie landed on the table to the Captain's left. He bobbed his head and waddled to the edge before reaching out his bill and butting Captain Black's shoulder.

CC's eyes threatened to pop from their sockets if she spread them any wider. "Wow. Wait'll I tell my friends I saw pirates with a pet pelican." She took her parents' hands and pulled them toward the group of kids watching Captain Black interact with Bernie.

Darcy grinned and popped upright. A regular jack-in-the-box, that one. Never could sit still for long. Drove their teachers crazy, and since they were all homeschooled together, Nigel had been privy to every moment of Darcy's immense personality.

She elbowed Nigel in the ribs and wiggled her heavily penciled eyebrows. Her pirate makeup never ceased to amuse as she always went over the top with heavy eyeliner and super thick eyebrows. Her lips were scarlet today, something he'd been trying to avoid noticing since she stepped aboard just before sunrise.

Nigel nudged her back and cackled when she pursed her lips in a pout. Her straight, black hair teased her cheeks as the wind whipped over the bow. He liked her curls better. The days she let the natural curls spring around her face in long ringlets, he ached to twist one around his fingers. Darcy thought the curls made her look too much like her ancestor, the infamous pirate Anne Bonny. She despised the legacy Bonny'd left behind and always looked for a way to separate herself from her history. Hard to do when your dad operated a pirate boat tour that regaled tourists with pirate legends.

Nigel's fake dreads scratched against his neck, a familiar

sensation after so many years aboard ship. The familiar silence caressed his soul with a lover's touch. Too bad he could never tell Darcy how much he loved every piece of her past and her present. Or how much he longed to become part of her future. She'd become his treasure so long ago there wasn't a time in his memory when he'd not been in love with her.

"I'm always surprised how good you are with the kids." Darcy stuck her thumbs in her leather belt and rocked back on her heels.

"You shouldn't be. I love kids. They're the reason I'm out here sweating to death in a made-up pirate costume." Nigel mimicked her stance, his cutlass hilts bumping against his wrists and bringing him fully back to where they stood and the woman he could never have. "You should go out with us more. Most of this new crew doesn't even know who you are."

Darcy's gaze jumped to meet his, her blue eyes narrowing to slits. "And I don't want them to know. I don't want special treatment because Dad owns the *Treasure*."

"Best not let them see you slacking then." Nigel darted into the swarm of pirates dancing around the deck. Jerking his blunted cutlass from his waist, he punched it into the air, hooked elbows with one of the crew and joined in the ruckus of shouts and cheers.

Overhead, the bell clanged a warning. Bernie added a squawk to the clamor as pirates scrambled across the deck. Their tour came to an end, as Mimosa's dock drifted into sight. Captain Black nodded to Nigel, and he moved toward the cannon on the starboard deck. With a quick motion, he ignited the gunpowder and sent a deck-shuddering boom across the empty ocean. Cheers erupted from the crew and their guests. Even CC jumped up and down and waved in wild circles.

Captain Black steered them with an expert hand, and they bumped against the dock with barely a jostle. One of the new crew members settled the gangplank, then another strung up the rope for passengers to grasp as they made their way down the solid walkway.

Nigel scanned the docks, keeping track of guests as they left the *Treasure* and returned to Mimosa, where they could find almost anything a vacationer could ask for. A flash of white and gray, accompanied by an undeniably familiar bark pulled him from the deck and toward Mel, his friendly dog groomer, who held his canine's leash with a firm grip.

Darcy ran past him and fell to her knees in front of Shep, Nigel's Old English Sheepdog. Her arms wrapped around Shep, who woofed and tried to slobber his way through the layers of makeup. Darcy laughed and leaned away from the doggy advances.

Nigel staggered to a stop as every muscle tightened with desire.

Mel passed the leash over to Darcy and stalked toward Nigel. She halted less than a foot away and lowered her sunglasses, unleashing a full glare.

"Come on, Mel. Don't give me that look. It was an emergency."

"Picking up your dog on Elnora, grooming him, and spending hours on the ferry to bring him to you on *Mimosa* is not an emergency." Mel crossed her arms and practically sizzled with each word.

Nigel offered his sincerest puppy dog face.

Before he could get a word out, Mel sliced through the air with her hand. "No. Don't give me that look. I'm mad at you." Her voice cracked on the last word as a grin wiggled loose. Shep barked again, drawing Mel's attention.

Nigel pitched his voice low enough Darcy wouldn't hear. "Mr. Riggins is threatening eviction if Shep doesn't stop barking and digging holes under the fence." His hands worried the sash around his waist, twisting the red cotton into a knot.

"This is ridiculous, Nigel. You should tell Darcy what's going on. Surely, she can help you. It's her own father making your life miserable. What I can't understand, is why?"

A crowd of people converged around them, the next group of passengers amassing at the gangplank. An elderly man bumped Darcy, almost knocking her to the ground. Nigel elbowed his way through the crowd before Mel could press her interrogation. Telling Darcy her father wanted Nigel out of her life was out of the question. Darcy would demand to know why, much as Mel had. More. Darcy would not let well enough alone. She'd been his best friend since they met in first grade. Her sense of justice would drive her to investigate. Nigel could never let her learn the truth.

Made in the USA
Coppell, TX
26 August 2022

82097065R00120